By Peter Burnett

The Machine Doctor
Odium
The Supper Book
#freetopiary: An Occupy Romance

Peter Burnett
studiogame.peterburnett.info

Published by Fledgling Press 2012
fledglingpress.co.uk

Cover design by Graeme Clarke
Set in Bembo by Gerry Hillman

Printed and bound by
Martins the Printers
Berwick Upon Tweed
TD15 1RS

ISBN: 9781905916580

Art is a PRETENSION warmed by the TIMIDITY of the urinary basin, the hysteria born in The Studio.

Tristan Tzara

The exchange between what one / puts on view [the whole / setting up to put on view (all areas)] / and the glacial regard of the public (which sees /and forgets immediately) / Very often / this exchange has the value / of an infra thin separation / (meaning that the more / a thing is admired / and looked at the less there is an inf. T. / sep).

Marcel Duchamp, Notes, note 101

To Arlene

The Studio Game

1

☐   Liska and I lay in a heap. We lay like that all morning. In the darkness it had been like being dead but now we were alive the light hurt. We'd been testing the water, seeing if we could do it — seeing if we would do it — up until the moment when we did do it. I had typed a suicide note on the computer before we'd gone to sleep but I'd been drunk. The printed note said:

> Liska and I are leaving before daily life consumes us.
> Artists need to make a statement about art by making
> a statement about themselves as artists, and that is what
> we are doing. That's our private opinion. Goofbye.

In the blurred outlines of my memory I remembered the few attempts we'd made at these notes in the past and although this one was at least concise, it would have been a horrible way to go out — on a typo.

> cf. Alberto Greco : *Notes* (1965) The artist overdosed
> on barbiturates and left notes describing how he felt —
> for as long as was physically possible for him to do so.

I slept in my clothes with the Sunday newspapers spread over the blankets and the curtains drawn tight. When the lights came on it was Liska who woke me and I rose to find her staring into the caked and blistered oil paint I'd spread across my last canvas. An image of the sea that I'd worked on the day before. It was supposed to have been my final painting but it looked like I had a few more works left in me.

"I still love you," said Liska.

Everything was delineated and etched in our poor bedroom — even the broken wardrobe had an eternal cast about it. The windows rattled to the sound of a passing siren, the usual dull routine of a provincial town at the edge of the world. It was Aberdeen and we'd been fools to try and leave it.

"Let's have a drink," I said, but the sweetness that had occupied my mind when we had made our death pact was long gone.

"Where's the bottle?" asked Liska, and she dug her hands under the covers for the wine. I made a clumsy attempt to claim it, but Liska had been too fast.

I pretended to read the newspaper. (ART MORE PASSIONATE THAN PASTORAL — read the headline in the review section — followed by the weekly cataract of flowery horseshit that I was as usual, unable to stomach.)

"I saw things when I was dead and now I want to paint," said Liska.

I was jealous of her energy and her will to keep going. Everything she did was about making art.

Liska finished the bottle and I got out of bed to show her the latest from the newspaper, the profiles of some upcoming artists. There are so many artists out there but when you're young you believe yourself to be better than all of them. As an experiment I listed the names of every artist in the paper — some were famous, some were not, some dead and some were still going strong. I groaned and turned the pages, wondering when it would be my turn to be in the review section. Liska and I played the same game each weekend. I read out the name of every artist who was featured in the paper, and we outdid each other with drunken comments.

Such as — Andy Warhol — wanker / Jeff Koons — bollocks / Basquiat — has to be the worstest of them all / give me that bottle / Gordon Take — talentless poop-4-brains / Damien Hurst — did you know that his name is an anagram of RUDE SHIT MAN? / you'll need to go out and get more wine / Tracey Emin — for fuck's sake / Joseph Gram — the nerve of that prick / Martin Michie — sell-out! / Jake and Dinos Chapman — asswipe trash / Gavin Turk — the artist's worst enemy — everything he's done has been done before, most of it by Duchamp! / I know that, in fact I pointed it out to you SHITFISH! / Rachael Whiteread — poisoner of wells / Douglas Hastie —salamander ass, caterpillar ass pervert — and also a poisoner of wells / Martin Creed — DID THE ALIENS FORGET TO REMOVE THE ANAL PROBE — or what, huh? / anyway that's not how you spell Hirst — it's H I — not H U / so 'Ride Shit Man' then! / what does 'Ride Shit' mean? / I don't know — it's your anagram — just go to the shop and get more wine okay?

"Why don't you go?"

"Maybe I will."

"Go then."

With the wine decision made, Liska and I moved closer for the big makeup. I took Liska in my dirty baboon hands and we kissed, our lips brushing against each other as a signal of something tender.

It was a typical weekend, during which we painted, drank, set the world to rights, and attempted suicide. For me it was one of those days when I felt that in a world, which is almost entirely gagged, shackled and manacled, being an artist was the greatest of all luxuries. Our aim was fame, because we believed that celebrity would somehow justify our work, and when you're young, that kind of thing is important.

"I love you," I said.

"I love you more," said Liska

The newspaper finished with, I departed like a thirsty homing-rat for the corner shop where I shovelled money onto the counter for more wine. We returned to work and there was further drinking, more kissing, and a good deal of musing over how famous we might be one day. If only someone would value our pictures.

2

■ On our first date, Liska and I ran away from home. Two hundred miles sunward of the spot where Liska would in due course drown, my highest hopes were realised when she agreed with me that we had no future worth living for. As we left on that first date, Liska stood in the doorway of her flat and hugged a bottle of wine, which rang with a pleasant slosh. Her earrings jingled slightly, drawing my attention to the red-rusty streaks of colour in her hair. I asked if I could look at her paintings but she shook her head.

"They're not to be seen," she said. "You can damage a work of art just by looking at it."

While Liska drank the wine I twiddled my locks, wondering what she meant by her last fantastic statement.

"How can you destroy a picture just by looking at it?" I asked.

Liska explained. "You'd say something pointless like — *I like the use of colour* — and that would be the end of it."

We left Liska's flat and passed the key through the letterbox on a string. I noticed the postcards she'd taped to her door, Vincent van Gogh's yellow lantern lights and a black square by that other famous bad-luck case, Mark Rothko. We gazed on these primitive images, sure that as young artists we would one day match these geniuses' abilities and fame. Quietly the images grew on us until we squeezed together in a hug.

This is the first kiss, I thought, and I delighted in our sudden closeness. I was caught in the purity of the moment and the trembling touch of our lips left a glow in my head.

Liska jumped from the step and froze. The postcards had reminded her of our idea that dead artists fared better than living ones. The thought was never far from our minds.

"Do you think suicide is the ultimate work of art?" she asked.

"It could be," I answered. "It's certainly where conceptual art has been heading."

We walked out of the city of Aberdeen, until we stopped at Balmedie Beach. On the North Sea a ferry sat like a fieldstone on the horizon, and the thought occurred again.

"People like their artists dead," said Liska.

"I'm afraid so," I admitted.

Liska squinted, the sunlight mobile on her face, and she gave an oblique stare to the sea. We were near the golf course at Balmedie, and we walked its boundary like we were visitors from outer space. The sun was a speck of light and we followed it. We crossed a hard field to where the sound of the dual carriageway was sifted by the trees. Here, the soft voice of the wind combined with the rise and fall of passing traffic. The horn of a lorry sang two notes and the sound paused before the silence drew in again.

"Would you like to exhibit your paintings before you die?" asked Liska.

"Of course I would," I said. "What would be the point otherwise?"

"You tell me," she said mysteriously.

"I'd like to be famous," I said. "That's why we do it, isn't it?"

I poked my foot at a nearby hedge.

"I'd like all my paintings to be displayed at the same time," said Liska — and I saw that unshakeable smile of hers. "When all my paintings are done," she said, "I want them to be shown together — otherwise not at all. Then I'll kill myself and turn into an overpriced dead-artist, while bollocks journalists write brilliant things about me."

A track led past the peaked roofs of the golf course hotel and we kept going, past several deserted farmhouses and into the north. We were on a disused road, an avenue at the perimeter of the bay, both of us following the rough outline of the hedges in the dark. The clouds drifted over the sea into deeper backwaters of darkness. We could see the lights of a starry village to the north and I remembered a picnic spot from long before. The beach was empty and the silence was pouring from the sky as we picked our way forward. It was dark but I could still see Liska's smile.

That smile has followed me everywhere. It's come beaming out of dreams and has risen from the sunken heart of the sea. There is testimony in that smile of Liska's, a confirmation that her suicide was correct.

With our blankets out we began upon the wine. The sea became bluer in the night and the water glowed in the dun. We drank, and though the air was black, I smiled and could see Liska smile back.

3

☐ When I had the courage of a good idea I painted at the studio run by Heery the Hippie of Multiple Solitude. Heery's face possessed all the mischief of a seaport rent-boy and his Aberdeen studio was filled with canvases, rescued furniture and the industrial rubbish that he and the other artists had collected from the harbour. It was in this studio that Heery invented a photographic process by which he captured the phantoms of his mind. Once Heery had collected mirrors, charts and other junk for his mind-phantom-photograph, he would expose photographic sheets and dance his arms before them, although all the observer could see at the end of the process were papers tinted with varied shades of black.

Some days everyone in the studio was involved in Heery's photographic creations and we all stopped what we were doing to help him. All Heery had to do was to grab two phantoms each week and the studio was happy. His was a misleading example. Heery set up a reflective sheet, tied his hair back and crossed his legs. Light blasted off the sky into the space above Heery's head where the phantoms would gather — and Heery would mentally 'photograph' the emptiness when he felt his spirit move. Heery was convinced that if you collected enough cerebral energy in the right place then art might happen of its own accord.

Heery the Hippie of Multiple Solitude had collected then — out of his interest in art creating itself — several hundred photographs of his own phantoms. He exhibited his shadowy photographs only once, but they were not liked. Twenty black photographs with mystical first person narratives attached were never going to make Heery's fortune, but we artists continued to champion the starving artist Heery nonetheless.

Heery the Hippie of Multiple Solitude is not in Aberdeen any more. They didn't like his clothes. His beard was matted with dreadlocks like pewter lumps. The Aberdonians didn't like the fact that Heery's ideas were all hatched in the slum of the New Age, which they saw as dangerous, with its talk of energies and crystal manipulations. Don't imagine that Heery's beard would have mattered if he were the greatest artist of his era. It wouldn't have. Heery was the self-styled pioneer of Modificationism and worse, he was an anarchist from the Islands of the Gaels. The subject matter was not at issue. Elsewhere artists were pickling animals and selling pots of urine. Piss was highly popular as a matter of fact, as were various other bodily fluids, including blood — even though all of that had been done before, and done before that. Solid cast plaster surrogates of baby's hands and feet were in style in London and Liverpool, and a rat carcass won a national prize. The price of artists' dung was up to 10 grand a slice and a slush of vomit had been voted as 'our nation's signature'. You could buy a crumpled paper ball for £100, and an artist could earn up to 400 times that for exhibiting an empty room — which the public found profound and challenging, every time.

> cf. Yves Klein : *The Specialization of Sensibility in the Raw Material State into Stabilized Pictorial Sensibility, The Void* (1958) Klein removed everything in the gallery space, painted every surface white, and then staged an elaborate entrance procedure for the opening night at which he declared his art to be invisible.

The problem was not with Heery's work. Doubtless you would have said that Heery was a nice boy. Heery was the Hippie of Multiple Solitude after all.

But Heery was the sort of artist who felt it necessary to antagonise society instead of amuse it. Some mean instinct of self-preservation had obliged Heery to try and get money for what he did, but of course he should have known better. He would have never enjoyed fame anyway.

Liska was already working on her series of artworks that would never be exhibited, and the other artists in our studio had said that it was a crime that, like Heery, Liska had been ignored. Liska didn't mind being ignored because her plan was to finish her entire output and have it staged as one single exhibit. She had in mind 58 pieces and wanted to get every one of them right before she retired at the age of 25.

Heery was the focal point of our gang however and the tablet of memory for that year is marked with his rejection by the art agent Anna Lunken: the only art agent in all of Aberdeen.

Here she is now, the art agent Anna Lunken, the star of this story, her mouth paused and stretched in the middle of a word

"Aah —"

That was how I painted her, at least. Anna Lunken had heard about Heery's phantom images and had picked her way up the stairs to the studio, giving Heery's black photographs five minutes of her time. It is said that Anna Lunken looked on Heery's pictures with sympathy and asked if there were any more. When she was told that there were not, that was when Anna Lunken saw Liska, my love.

Nothing was sold that day but art was on the move. Some terms and conditions were talked and while Heery returned to photographing imaginary bubbles, Liska and I read some conditions of sale in a funny piece of paper that Anna Lunken had left — a piece of paper amusingly called a contract.

■   The same art shows were launching everywhere, with the same heathen rites performed using price tags, wine glasses and catalogues. The project was domestication, living artists enslaved to a mass of gallery-goers.

Anna Lunken the art agent was interested in artists as much as art. When in the galleria, Anna Lunken moved from picture to picture and said a few words of praise. In every alcove in Aberdeen's galleries there was a work of art with a price tag that concealed its deficiencies. Whether it was a female nude or a digital installation, Anna Lunken didn't hesitate to bustle forward and find out who the artist was.

As a side dish to our regular daily ration of self-torment, Liska and I were always trying to think of another word for artist — but we weren't allowed to use any alternatives by our agent Anna Lunken. We had to be called 'artists' and there was no getting away from it. Even the phrase cultural anchorite was banned. Nor was Liska permitted to be a daubster, nor a smudger, and nor was I permitted to be a guerrilla ontologist nor an easler. Liska and I thought of more interesting and often uglier words for art but could find no English expression to suggest the temperamental inclination we had towards painting all day, drinking wine, and throwing ourselves in the sea.

> cf : earthlings, parties, mart, tarts, participation, Artaud, cartoon, artificial, partnership, impartial, Barthes, Eckhart, hamartia, Hartley, Bartlett, McCarthy, Hartung, Artschwager, Baumgarten, del Sarto, Fra Bartolommeo, Martini, Artemisia Gentileschi, Hogarth, Peter Martyr, Martial, Lockhart, *Sartor Resartus*, Mary Barton, Moriarty, *Morte d' Arthur,*

Amy Robsart, The Quarterly Review, *Parthenophil and Parthenope*, Martinmas (normally, the time of slaughter!) — and so on. For *art*, read *clart*!

See also Page 187 of this novel — Heery said this works much better in Gaelic — and he was correct!

"Are you really an artist?" Liska once asked me.

"Uh huh," I said.

"?"

"I really think I am!" I said.

It was the difference between beauty and ordure. All an artist needed to do was conceptualise + realise and then sweet, sweet art was made. After that it was a case of get thee to the gallery, and once in there you were an artist, on the basis of general agreement.

That great excretion that began so long ago — it deepens like a shelf of junk mail. All that wind and hiccup, it needs to be expelled, and I can never help thinking that artists who have their work in galleries are somehow better than I am.

☐ "Of course they're better than you," said Liska. "Better paid and better organised. Better publicised and better at getting the best out of themselves. They're predators and they'll get at ya — one way or another, brother. It's like that. And that's the way it is."

West of Aberdeen, human figures sat abstractedly at a series of waterside hotels, doves called sweet nothings from the trees and hysterical art-lovers drove motorcars towards the galleries in strange spasms of rage. On the North Deeside Road, a sign pointed to the Myrtle Gallery, a super-sized villa with a lawn that led to the black bank of Queen Victoria's favourite river.

With the nod from Anna Lunken, Liska and I had been invited to exhibit at the Myrtle Gallery by the promoters of the Baal's Beer annual show. It was our first opportunity and Liska volunteered five pieces, all of which were accepted. I did less well and neither of the two I had entered was chosen to be displayed.

Liska and I entered the gallery and picked up our glasses of wine. Heery was there, magicking free beers into his rucksack, his usual ploy. That year, the Baal's Beer shows in Scotland were dominated by Martin Michie whose photographs showed what he referred to as the 'dark dust lanes that are prominent in the light.' It was whispered that Michie could win the Baal's Beer Prize, a rumour that had heightened interest among the well-clad guests present that day.

The sponsor from Baal's Beer had seen us stowing his company's free drinks into Heery's bag, and he tutted as he passed. Heery offered him a beer from his pocket and the sponsor looked so oppressively cold that the crusted glass of his spectacles iced over. We local artists were unmannered loafers — typically unsophisticated — and what we thought funny the established beings of the art world did not.

Liska and I followed Anna Lunken through the crowd, amused

that, as an agent, she seemed to adore everything on display. Anna Lunken was excited as hell to be in the presence of art and was passionate about everything in equal measure. The result was pseudology — a science of halves, operating on the principal that art is something to fill space on an otherwise boring wall. Anna Lunken's lips formed a carnation and she kissed the air and then the artist, while Liska and I circled nearby, seeking the vitalising agent of white wine.

By then we knew Anna Lunken by heart. Gold jacket like a life preserver — blood pumping into her fingers so that you wondered how she might ever remove her rings — ankles the texture of marshmallow, pearls like propitious stars around her neck — dauntless and yet compassionate expression, able to speak to both herself and a painting at the same time.

> cf. Duane Hanson : *Young Shopper* (1973) Polyester
> and fibreglass, polychromed in oil, with accessories,
> life size.

"So strong an emphasis on the ideals of harmony and precision," said Anna Lunken — and I had not the use of my tongue.

"Quite the most daring statement of our times," she said with a pained expression, which may, in any other circumstance, have suggested a grave ailment of the bladder.

Liska was surprised by this bold woman who eclipsed the room with her opinions.

"I've just sold four of your pictures," said Anna Lunken. "If you've got any more in your studio, then I know someone who'd like to see them."

Liska shook her head and put her nose back in her glass of wine. Anna Lunken continued to speak to Liska and myself, simultaneously addressing the gallery owners and a sponsor, managing to keep five people quiet at the same time.

"Few people appreciate the obvious necessity of art," she said.

Liska and I glanced at each other. One day standards of appreciation would decline so far that artists would refuse to sell anything at all. That was basically Liska's idea.

"As an art agent," said Anna Lunken, "it's my job to remind everybody of art's necessity — as well as making sure that everybody's happy."

Liska scraped at the floor with her shoe. I glanced out of the window as several cars pulled up, and from them more plutocrats beat a path towards the art. The suburbs were busy. Business was booming in the gourmet food stores, health clubs and private art galleries — everywhere, in short, that properly serviced the purified beings who had crash-landed there.

Martin Michie was photographed as he unknotted his tie and shuffled it around his neck. A journalist held a recording device in the air as Michie issued a few more of his trademark bitter ruminations against the dominance of the art scene by the so-called 'London galleries', and when he was through with this and ready for his next photograph, he emptied his pockets to flatten his jacket against his chest. Michie's wallet was the last thing to emerge, a leather slug of money that landed on the bar near where we stood. When Heery noticed the wallet he grabbed it and began to count the banknotes.

"What you gonna do?" I said.

"This wallet is a work of art," said Heery.

Of course Heery was drunk. The Baal's Beer had restored the humanity of his creative powers, whereby everything became art.

"We can keep the money," said Heery, "there's enough in here."

"Don't be silly," said Liska.

"Artist's money!" said Heery — and he began to speculate how much he could sell it for.

Heery counted the notes but Liska wasn't interested. Instead she looked at her own paintings with a rising doubt. As Diogenes realised that cups were irrelevant when he saw a dog drinking from a puddle, so Liska was about to discover the redundancy of galleries when she saw the locals lapping up her art. Liska had her epiphany as we all finished our wine and Heery offered us some notes from Michie's wallet, pleased that there'd been profit in the trip.

"Squarely," said Heery, "this event is for one group only — haters of art, as I perceive them — commercial management committees — buyers and sponsors with personal grudges — collectors and their bad taste."

Heery poked the words at me with an unabashed pronunciation and punctuated the message with his dirty smile. "They'll kill us all," he said.

The three of us moved on to the next white space where political messages were being projected on to several sheaves of corn. The crania of the guests were arranged in a semi-circle around these sheaves of corn while the artists stood like ornamental courtiers, being asked questions such as:

"Where do you get your ideas?" and

"Where do you see yourself in five years time?"

That companies like Baal's Beer had become arbiters of art was bad enough — but the hostile organs of material civilisation were asking artists to be salespeople too.

Anna Lunken worked the room, filling people's glasses with balancing movements on her arches. Her hyperbole was without end and when she sat, she crossed her legs and confessed that it was a matter of embarrassment that multinational companies were not pulling their weight in terms of purchase. Seizing the moment, Anna Lunken then proceeded to sell the undisturbed interior of Martin Michie's mind (a painted plastic bucket) to someone who didn't even realise that it was a work of art.

Anna Lunken continued selling art for the next hour. She presented artists to buyers and buyers to paintings, and the artists bowed in all directions, in case they should be found wanting in some respect. Nobody minded if the art was any good or not, because all of it was seasoned with a few words of praise.

"I want to tell you," said Anna Lunken addressing some guests from a great insurance company, "that art can increase productivity by enlivening the work place. Our consciousness may rarely register it, but art in the workplace can make a great difference to workers' concentration and attitude."

This was as barrel-banging as it got.

Insert your own excuse not to buy.

Liska slipped away for another drink and was brushed on the shoulder by Anna Lunken.

"Your pictures are exceptional," said Anna Lunken. "I'd like to see some more as soon as I can. The colours are strong. They have rhythm and unity."

Liska's tactic was to nod when people were speaking because she believed it gave them the impression she was listening. Liska wasn't listening, however, and her plan was to get back to the studio with just enough drink inside her to splash another picture before bed. The gallery was the unhappy end point of the artistic process and it didn't pay for either of us to spend too long there once we'd had our fill of booze.

"Tell me," Anna Lunken said to Liska, "I keep seeing you and Guy hold hands. Does that mean that you are actually a couple?"

The Guy she meant was me.

"It actually does — and we are a couple," said Liska, much to Anna Lunken's delight.

Something in me warmed to Anna Lunken, as if she might just understand our project — but I may have been drunk on Baal's.

"And you're a painter too!" said Anna Lunken to me. I worked the question over but didn't answer.

Anna Lunken carried on talking, the three of us couched in the bright, end quarter of the Myrtle Gallery. I felt awkward — and a chill upon my cheek confirmed this feeling for me.

I looked around and saw exactly what it was. Joseph Gram.

6

■ The choking fumes of falsehood will be expressed from this point on in the figure of Joseph Gram. That day at the Myrtle Gallery in Aberdeen, Joseph Gram was showing several lead slabs inscribed with his name in gold paint. Gram passed me in a tall grey suit, and I heard him say the words 'New York' and the phrase 'broad conceptual gap'. One of the slabs included a slot for a light bulb while the only distinguishing mark on the second was Gram's gold signature.

"It's the elegance she has," said Anna Lunken.

She was speaking about Liska and I realised in time to thank her.

"I can advise you both on style," said Anna Lunken. "I always know what's coming into fashion and what's becoming old hat crap."

"I see," I said.

Old hat crap sounded disgusting, and unpleasant for your hair.

Anna Lunken's eyes opened like camera lenses for more light while I drank more sleep-provoking Baal's Beer. In the revolutionary state brought on by the combination of beer and art, all that I could feel were the wheels and gears of conspiracy. Joseph Gram eyed me like a wood wasp, and then looked Liska up and down, while the other artists gathered in the corner, as shadowy as rats. It's true that I could never have come up with anything like Joseph Gram's lead slabs — and it was true that he was brave to display them — but I didn't care for Joseph Gram at that moment. Liska and I were being initiated into the scene by Anna Lunken and I wondered if Gram had received the same treatment at some point in his life.

"How much are you selling these paintings for?"

Anna Lunken's questions contended with the saucer-eyed conversation in the rest of the gallery.

"I'm not interested in sales," said Liska — and she stared at a foul metal mandrake erected in the centre of the room.

"I'm sorry?" said Anna Lunken, and she swivelled two ball-bearing eyes.

"My paintings are not for sale," said Liska. "I don't know why you thought you could sell them — but none of my work is available."

Anna Lunken took this idea on board as if it was part of something very clever indeed.

She whacked back her wine.

"I'm sorry to hear that your work's not available," said Anna Lunken and after a moment added: "That aside, I'd really like to offer them to my client."

I could see the fascination, the way that Anna Lunken shot me a coy glance. Anna Lunken knew she could get the pictures one way or another and she admired Liska for making them unavailable. Liska wasn't joking but Anna Lunken knew a novelty when she saw it. This was, in fact, just the sort of tactic that young artists should use — because now Anna Lunken was staring longingly at one of Liska's pictures, like a child staring at Santa's sack.

"I know what price I can get you for this, for example," said Anna Lunken. "Even if it's not for sale."

Liska found this funny and tugged her baggy trousers. Anna Lunken looked at me again. She was thinking of the novelty. I remembered something Liska had said — *if art is a digestive process, then the art gallery is the arse where those who can afford it sift through the shit*. I folded my arms and glanced at the Joseph Gram lead block. It became worse each time I saw it.

"I really must speak to the sponsor," said Anna Lunken and she shifted at high speed across the gallery to the door, past people with their drinks at chest height.

"What do you think she's saying?" asked Liska.

Anna Lunken was speaking to the sponsors.

"She's asking what's going on," I said.

A few seconds into Anna Lunken's quiet outpouring, every person in her group, including Joseph Gram, turned to look at us. Each darksome face showed the same doubt at that moment, like a jury en route to a bad verdict.

"Let's get going," said Liska. "The white wine is urine. I need some red and then to do some painting. Shall we get out of here?"

I would have said yes but a delegation was making its way over and it looked like Liska was for the grill. I pointed at the party of critics and buyers, a group led by Anna Lunken and the artist Joseph Gram.

"They're coming to ask you what you're playing at," I said. "I hope you're ready."

We watched as this pod of gallery-goers approached. Anna Lunken and Joseph Gram had their eyes on us all right, but they still found time to stop and make inquisition of a sculpture by Douglas Hastie, who was slurring through his wet facial hair nearby. Douglas Hastie looked like he was explaining the act of sex to a terrified young couple, but he was interrupted by Anna Lunken who invited him to join the delegation.

"Is that really Douglas Hastie?" I asked. "He looks like a fucking drunk."

"It's him all right," said Liska.

Douglas Hastie was an ageing automaton of the art scene who inspected life through a cracked and cynical lens. A grant cheque had funded his last trip to Greece and he'd returned to show his extremely lame *Photo Transformations* to a public that had responded with customary excess.

"You must be Liska," said one of the sponsors when the party arrived.

The sponsor's voice probed Liska in the same way that police speak to uncertain witnesses. The sponsor was the higher authority to which Anna Lunken had resorted after having had her money turned down.

"I'm sorry," said the sponsor, "but exhibiting here means that contractually your work is for sale. And very promising work it is too."

Liska put her glass of urine down and stuck her hands in her pockets.

I breathed in Joseph Gram's contempt. Gram had glanced at me when the sponsor had called Liska *promising* because they'd said that about him one time. Years later and Gram was in dark union with the art world, and his work hung in the foyers of several oil companies and computer firms. Joseph Gram had run the course, and had paintings in the offices of some of the most repulsive interbeastiaries in the land.

"Your paintings are sold," said the sponsor to Liska, and he turned his head through an arc to ensure that everybody had heard.

"Is that what the little red dot is for?" asked Liska, and all the monkeys laughed as if Liska were the greatest wit of the season. Liska laughed too, and Anna Lunken joined in, although her face was taut and anxious. Even Joseph Gram was laughing.

"Look," said the sponsor. "I'm sorry about the misunderstanding, but please, let's have a chat afterwards. If you really want your paintings back then I suppose that can happen. The important thing is that you and Anna are getting on. I think Anna should bring some more of your work here. We're fascinated to see what else you've got."

"I guess so," said Liska — but I knew that meant a *no*. When Liska was ready to show her work, she wanted them to be seen all at the same time.

"The thing is," said Liska, "none of my paintings are for sale. If you like my paintings then you can view them all at once when they're ready. All my work is going to form one piece."

"What is this?" asked Anna Lunken. Her snout opened and farted out this stupid question.

"You're selling *all* your artworks at the same time?" asked Joseph

Gram. He pretended not to be interested but I could see that he had smelled a gimmick and was keen to test it out.

"I didn't say selling," said Liska. "I'd still like them all to be considered as one, however."

The attention didn't frighten her. These people were a group of single separates who behaved as one strange eye, a nematode hovering in inspection of the potential alien.

"How many artworks will there be?" asked Gram.

"I'm thinking of 58," said Liska.

A hush confronted the circle of art-likers when they understood what was happening with my Liska. Liska's work was off limits until the entire output was ready. Then, if they were lucky, it may be for sale *en bloc*.

"I have to destroy these pictures now you've seen them," said Liska — and Anna Lunken spilled her wine.

"They're sold!" she said again, almost in a shout.

The group before us exchanged glances. The sponsor was amused by Liska's tactic and Joseph Gram was irritated. Liska was in earnest about her work not being seen by anybody but to them it was only a ploy — a neat concept, as your average journalist might say. A crazy, new, all-defying concept.

"I have to destroy these pictures now that you've seen them," repeated Liska, and she spun a cigarette in her hand, readying for the exit.

"You bloody bitch," whispered Douglas Hastie, his face over-red for his elderly heart. The art student who accompanied Douglas Hastie looked scared stiff. As Liska glanced back at Hastie, the old pervert in the metallic white beard, he of the many topless young ladies (on horseback I have heard!) growled something else, although conversation rose again like a warm spring, to cover his bad manners.

7

☐　Beer sponsors art and keeps the powers of expression in thrall to the arbiters who sell a million pints a month. It makes both art and beer more tolerable and ensures a general intoxication in the galleries. The artists keep their fingers crossed that the buyers will be as drunk as they are, and the winner of the Baal's Beer Prize stands for a photo with the well-known 'world-is-my-oyster' smile. Beer gives you a pain and so does genius, so the association dings in the brain. Our national airline has supported several revivals and this is how Munch came back for his last appearance, hot on the trail of Klee's shampoo. Dali's comeback was part-funded by some petrol-pushing poisoner, proof that 'care dollars' make clean money. Tax walls are jumped when sponsorship deals are made and the public make the obvious connection between art and consumption. One year, Van Gogh paintings were toured with sponsorship money from one of the big names in cheese — here in Scotland — cheese. Strangely, not one person in any gallery complained, they're so used to the fact that art and cheese should go together. Audiences understand that any form of life will hook up with the frostiest of commercial cousins in order that both should thrive.

    cf. Wendy Ackman : *I Was Only Being Ironic* (2002)
    video, family, emptiness.

Art crumbling from the inside smells of what it's really made of. Blame Baal's Beer for calling the people it sponsors 'artists' because they're given the chance to show their own fermented produce in a space designated as an 'art gallery'.

cf. Franz Ronco : *This Work is Stupid, Because Life is Stupid* (1997) A piece of wood impaled in a rubber doll.

Selling artwork in this climate became a test for Liska, myself and the rest of us. It became so difficult for some people to make real art that the art prizes became a joke, as did the art prices. Most artists starved and moaned while a couple chosen at random became celebrities and millionaires.

cf. John Zemon : *Anti-Saloon* (1999) Mixed media installation, refuse specific to the site of installation, broken technology and collected litter.

Did you ever see a painter stare at her tube of paint? They do it plenty. In the art schools they're doing it right now, looking into the nozzle of their paint tubes. They're asking — how will I turn this multi-coloured squish into my art? A density comes over their faces — a wonder at all the bog shit — and then another voice kicks in — and that voice is the blank canvas from which your average creative can begin.

Artists have realised that art is second-rate stuff, not much higher than advertising and no closer to God than a packet of Cheese and Onion. In this world of means and ends, where artists are caught like fossils in a shale of cash, I know for a fact that the word 'art' has helped to price an endless mountain of work that is patently anything but. The burden of this book is to explain all this away. The reason Liska and I kept away from dealers right until the end was that we were able to revoke the shame so many artists feel when they hook up with their commercial betters and face the crudities of the market.

Liska was not impressed with public taste and that's why she had these ideas — first that none of her work should be for sale — and second that none of her work would be finished until it was all finished.

The third pillar of Liska's program had already been demonstrated to Anna Lunken in the gallery — but Liska really believed that if the bourjoissy so much as *looked* at her work, then that work would be destroyed.

Is it really possible (as Joseph Gram stated at Liska's funeral) that art was being annihilated by commercial tastes and trends?

■ So, wonder that we would try and live like this. Money isn't just the basis for survival but it's also the constituting force of social order. If we were to get money then we had to do something better than take a moral stance, and yet we felt the need to exclude ourselves from the art market. The dry, matter of fact actions of survival were paying the rent, eating, drinking and buying materials. Putting eating to one side, because we often did without it, the hazards of life were listed as simple arithmetic, but they still needed to be paid for. Everything ran in circles, and yet Liska and I still felt there was something art could do to save the situation.

>   cf. Hans Eels : *Subjectivité* (1999) in which the work is
>   the security guard hired to protect the work.

Conceptual Art: the bastard offspring of Sponsorship.
Sex and Violence: the overspill and catch-all themes of these undesirable movements.
The Studio Game: that which encourages conceptual art by making everything an irony.
Formalism: that which ridicules the benefits of modern living while fully benefiting from it.
The Gallery Show: that which beautifies our creations, culminating in the brute force of the over-hefty price tag.

"I'll finish my paintings and that's it," said Liska.
"What do you mean?" I asked.
"Once my paintings are finished then my life will end."
We were at the window of Heery's studio, viewing the turning sweep of Aberdeen harbour. Men pegged away at levers and vehicle

transports plodded to the shore. Liska and I lolled like connoisseurs of calm while shoreside, manual labour progressed nearby. The dual carriageway took a sharp corner below the studio window, and children ran terror-stricken between the lights on their way to school. The enemies of work were passivity and sloth, Liska and Guy, and we combated this ennui with painting and sculpture, replying promptly to our calling.

We admired the anxiety that was special to city life in Aberdeen. Satisfying labour began for everybody else at eight o'clock but when we worked, it barely seemed to be the same, because we were not being paid. For us, work meant painting and that meant echoing the collective sensibility, but the one thing it did not involve was income.

IN-COME. What a stupid word. It still however had to be accounted for,

☐   When it was time to meet the buyer who'd been interested in Liska's paintings, Anna Lunken asked us to dress as smartly as we could. We had all heard of Mr Sharma and the wonders he could produce in turning artists into financially viable entities — a most difficult proposition — and we agreed to go to his place of work to see what he was offering. As for smart, it was not a thing that we could manage. We took our quest to the charity shops, but even there were uselessly confined by our means.

There was art everywhere in Mr Sharma's office — art to aestheticise the material security of his company and art to prove that he had taste. Art had a few other functions but Mr Sharma wasn't used to them. He would never, for example, have considered art as an *investment* — a crudity he believed — and he would never sponsor an artist in order to meet a potential tax liability. Instead, Mr Sharma liked to make his artists commercially viable, although how he did this was a sacred mystery. The art in Mr Sharma's office had been selected on how well its shape and colour accorded to the space. His company was a firm of commodity managers, and behind the black hemisphere of their desks, men and women configured the price of something — I don't know what.

Here is a connection, I thought, horrified at my appearance in this sink of corporate strategy. Like many other offices, it was, as far as I could see, a graveyard of art and artists — in short, non-spaces domesticated with dead images.

Liska and I were seated beside Anna Lunken and were brought tea by assistants. There was a red seascape by Joseph Harper called *Modal Tides* and underneath, a print of the bed-ridden John Bellany, dreaming of the golden city of his fridge as a gang of hooded seabirds gave him the colourcast eye from the rocks outside his window.

Around the doors was more art — one called *White Writing* by Somebody Gordon and a zig-zag of shapes called *Pink Pink Prison*.

"I've become extraordinarily sensitive to painting," said Anna Lunken while we sat beneath this inevitably anodyne collection. Anna Lunken talked of *ongoing studio relationships*, and the jewels of her eyes were wet with delight.

"They have eight thousand square feet of empty wall space in the average office," she said, "and nobody is ever delegated to find art for it. Most of the art here is produced by Mr Sharma's own studio. Mr Sharma offers artists unlimited funding. It's all about talented young people."

A folder was produced and in it were the schematic explanations typical to business. We stared at the name of our benefactor, Mr Sharma, whose card rose out of this eddy of paper and was placed in both our hands.

"If you know Mr Sharma," said Anna Lunken, "you'll know that he's succeeded where everyone else has failed. His studio supports and nurtures artists while ensuring that the artists get paid. It's an entire experience."

Liska gripped my hand. Past the glare of fluorescent light a stylish woman pointed a light pen along some production targets. Shadows were flattened so there was no depth anywhere and both Liska and I were both thinking of the same thing — the suicidal last words of good old George Eastman:

To my friends — my work is done.
Why wait?

What else could make the synthetic world of the office real, I thought, other than the dream-created forces of art?

While we waited for Mr Sharma, Liska and myself did the honest thing and gazed at the pictures on the wall with the gravity of the pre-destined, and waited for the full detail of the economic performance that united artists with money, and money with art.

■ Mr Sharma was impressive. He closed his laptop with a slim brown finger and shook hands with Anna Lunken. Liska and I awaited our introduction. Mr Sharma's nose was like a needle and he gave us both a benign smile, demonstrating all the polish of a successful businessman. Anna Lunken bowed and the cleft of Mr Sharma's chin smiled.

"Liska and Guy, this is Mr Sharma," she said. "He runs the Aberdeen Artists' Studio."

Mr Sharma pressed my hand and said hello.

There was no getting past Mr Sharma's professional credentials when he flattened his hand in mine.

"It's nice to meet you both,' he said. "I can't wait to see more of your work, Liska. I'm sorry that my plan to buy some of it fell through."

Mr Sharma walked ahead and Liska and I pursed our lips and followed. We slid through to a meeting room where we sat in a window alcove. In nearby glass containers were more young business people whose forked tongues could be heard clicking in the sunlight.

"Mr Sharma has married art and business several times over!" said Anna Lunken. She referred again to the folder with the business plan which, if I remember it, was something as basic as:

I'd heard it before but it was never this funny. Mr Sharma was a dinosaur-shaped super-patron of the arts and the sudden earth-shuddering sound you heard was his pen hitting his chequebook in approval. Mr Sharma rested his arms on his chair, and sunbeams splayed across his head while we sat before his earthly radiance. He stroked his chin and pulled out some more papers.

"I'd love for both of you to work in my studio," he said. "The studio is funded by me. You're free to make whatever work you like, but it'll be mine to sell for you."

Mr Sharma was talking with an eminence that gave the impression of a prepared speech. He was not to be stopped.

"You can both work in the studio," he said. "There are painting facilities and pleasant accommodation. You can live there. It's a community, so you're always with like-minded souls."

One of Mr Sharma's brown hands was splayed before him, and as he made this last statement several cups of tea landed before us. The boy who brought our tea flinched as Mr Sharma smiled through the stalks of his teeth.

"Being is a chain," said Mr Sharma, "and there is no scale of values in this chain. There are no absolutes and no artist in my studio is obliged to do anything — all they do is work there. I also employ advisers and agents — I employ talent, in short."

A natural lull in the office. Neither Liska nor myself were breathing, Mr Sharma was saying nothing, and talk in the other rooms had stopped, like bullets in mid air. Anna Lunken applied a spade of sugar to her tea. There was a sparkle on the carriageway of the road outside and words died like they do sometimes, endowing the room with an awkward moment of inspection, when a cough or a hum can ignite a conversation. Not a person spoke and Mr Sharma sat back to look at us.

Liska pushed my arm.

I had expected various crude attempts at earnestness from Mr Sharma. He had invited me to a free ride in his artists' studio, but I was suspicious. Mr Sharma was a businessman and a profiteer on art — a mystery mixture — and Liska and I were invited to take part.

> cf. Tracey Emin : *Exorcism of the Last Painting I Ever Made* (1996) installation including 14 paintings, 78 drawings, 5 body prints, numerous painted items, art supplies, personal items, 1 bed and mattress and various other items of furniture, 1 radio and CD player, 9 music CDs, various newspapers and magazines — and numerous kitchen and food supplies. [For a complete inventory of the installation, please contact the department]. Trace locked herself up like a mad life model, and people paid to peep through tiny holes and watch her work.

It was all we could eat — it was our materials for free — no rent to pay — and all of our outpouring to be sold by Mr Sharma. I wondered if it really worked like that. Looking at the walls I wouldn't have said that what Mr Sharma's studio had produced was art, so much as a tired orgy of colour matching. What these efforts had to contend with was the scepticism of a shallow and uncertain time that could only ultimately judge a work of art by its price — high price being good, and lower price being less so. Liska had drawn a line between herself and that, and had nearly finished all the work she was ever going to do.

"There are facilities for everything," said Mr Sharma. "Both of you will have freedom and materials and you can even take part in your own marketing. I have buyers all over the world and a huge archive of work that's already been produced. I keep it in a warehouse."

It was clear then that the trick behind Mr Sharma's miracle was the artistic equivalent of spread-betting. Mr Sharma was making money from artists by having them make huge quantities of art for him and he was selling what he could and storing the rest. Likely, when the warehouse was full, he would insure it for several million and then burn it down. Mr Sharma's voice was a nasal wad of sound and I tried to listen. He was talking to me and yet the words were confused by the time they reached my ears.

"Are you saying that you sell what you can and stockpile the rest?" I asked.

"Some people want to sell their artwork — and other people want to sell the artwork of others," he said. "If you saw the studio you'd see 40 different young people engaged in different skills. It is in a very beautiful street in Aberdeen and it is a great place for artists to live and work, at least I'm sure that most of them think that. You know your history. The model is an ancient one. I am a benefactor and my business is what benefits. Your business too."

Mr Sharma closed his eyes. His head was a brown husk with hair on top, his smile calibrated with wrinkles from the sun.

"Is there anything you'd like to ask?" he said.

Liska and I looked at each other. I wanted to ask the same question again but I was having a love-moment. There was a delight to Liska's expression that didn't involve any of the questioning attached to other peoples' peering looks and I knew that she would never, not in a million years, accept Mr Sharma's offer.

"There's nothing at all to ask," she said, and her finger returned to her mouth.

"Show me some pictures then," asked Mr Sharma, "just for my curiosity."

Liska took out her notebook and Mr Sharma spread it on the table.

The pages of Liska's notebook turned, revealing pencil and dark ink drawings and writing of various strengths. Pages where a stubbier pen had drawn across certain black watercolours had once been so wet they crackled when Mr Sharma touched them. Images of blossoms — flowers entwined with reclining figures — figures spiralling loosely up the page like vines around elm, naked figures and broken coffins and tombs. Emblems: boys, birds and wings — a leftward horizon with an oblong sketch — clouds and seated figures, leafless trees and fish-men with facing-page explanations — designs and motifs that repeated in columns — studies of found objects and glass designs, sickbed scenes and a wild watercolour of someone drowning. Sketches of the sea, scores of variations on the same image. He finally handed it back.

"We are very interested," he said.

A third of the book had been sufficient for him.

"You should be aware," he said, "there are no commercial restraints at my studio. You could say that I act as an agent, if you want to look at it like that. All you need to know is that you won't have to bother with the money end of life. The artists in my studio don't need to go out hawking their work. This offers them an authenticity that I think you'll find admirable."

Mr Sharma spoke like he had an answer for everything, which he very likely did.

"I can show you something that you'll like," he said.

Mr Sharma closed one eye, as if he were a gunman lining up a shot. He motioned for us to come a little closer and we pulled up our chairs.

"Right into this eye," he said, and Liska leaned in, posing before Mr Sharma as if she were having her photograph taken. The marksman, Mr Sharma, moved nearer to Liska and closed his open eye.

I looked to Liska for a clue.

"This never fails," said Mr Sharma, "but it's best where there's more light, like in here. Now, is Liska ready?"

"Yes, I am," said Liska through her teeth.

Mr Sharma opened his left eye again, so sharply that I laughed.

"Hold it there," he said to Liska.

I was expecting something to happen but all I could see was Liska looking into Mr Sharma's eye.

"What is it?" I said after a moment — but the two of them were frozen.

"We'll do it for fifteen seconds," said Mr Sharma.

Liska smiled into Sharma's eye, watched by Anna Lunken and myself. Fifteen seconds is a long time in the passage of the Universe. Whole works of art can be painted and viewed, burned and rediscovered. The same works of art can be translated and disseminated and then buried again, all in this time. In fifteen seconds a person can die or be born, that goes without saying. And I waited for something to move, or for any of these things to happen. I was consciously aware of the amusing fact that nothing was happening at all — nothing in the scale that the Universe truly requires of man. There was a conversation nearby and a telephone rang.

"OK," said Mr Sharma, and he closed his eyes and sat back in his chair.

Liska took my hand and squeezed it. Mr Sharma was utterly still, with both eyes shut.

"You have to look in my eye now, Guy," said Mr Sharma, his eyes still closed. "You've got to look for the image there. You'll see it if you look right in, so you'll have to get up close."

"Go on," said Liska — and she let go of my hand.

I looked to Liska and she indicated Mr Sharma's face where I was expected to spy into his eye. I crouched before Mr Sharma's face.

"Ready?" asked Mr Sharma, and I said that I was.

Mr Sharma opened his eye and I looked in.

Sometimes people ask *what is art?* — and what is not — and even though there are always opinions — nobody seems to know. On the whole, this weakness of definition confirms the opinion of the people who, on seeing art, say that it's not art at all but is in fact merely a toilet bowl placed in a gallery. I endorse any strictures against the readiness people have to make the stuff that we call art, but I would never detract from the key source that supports it. The toilet bowl happens to indicate a general artistic disgust with public taste, because, roughly speaking, it parodies every classical marble statue in the world. I expect that the same thing could be done in other art forms, including writing, if anyone were brave enough to court the unpopularity they'd face.

> cf. Dieter Roth : *Literaturwurst der Welt* (Literature Sausage of the World) (1969) Cut newspaper in sausage skin with water, fat, spices.

The photograph in Mr Sharma's eye was as memorable an image as I have ever seen. Liska was pictured in the luminous light of an interior sun. The uncomplicated image that Mr Sharma had snapped was an exhibit with no title, as multitudinous as anything I could have imagined. It was, in effect, a photograph — a light imprint that amounted to a shadow which lingered for several seconds on the screen of Mr Sharma's eye — but it was unmistakably Liska. I had no idea how this worked, but I can assure you that it did. The rags of light had formed an image of Liska in the eye of our would-be artistic patron — an image of art beauty. Liska's picture faded back into the flourishes of vein that had captured it and as I watched this happen, I realised that it had vanished forever.

"Did you see it?" asked Mr Sharma.

"I saw it," I said.

Mr Sharma smiled generously. The picture of Liska had vanished into the brown of his eye and I waited for his offer once again.

"So, I'll maybe see you at the studio?" he said, and we both said *Uh huh*.

It would have been unfair to tell Mr Sharma that we were planning anything else.

"The door to the studio is open," said Mr Sharma. "I'll leave you both to decide — but it would of course, be a delight to have you join us."

Leaving the office, we crossed the tarmac and walked Mr Sharma all the way his car, seeing him right to the steering wheel. A minute later and Mr Sharma drove off towards the town, where he carried out whatever secret work he thrived upon and Liska and I said goodbye to Anna Lunken and pottered back to the studio, amused with the works of others, but concentrated only on our own.

11

☐   So, wonder that we would try and live like this, scraping together enough time, strength, cash and patience to do a little painting. Anything, in fact, so that we didn't have to get jobs. Instead of seeking steady employment, Liska and I mulled upon the fine and final words of the poet Sara Teasdale, who died cold-hearted and by her own hand:

Tho' you should lean above me broken-hearted,
I shall not care.

A small amount of paint on the brush, and follow the last line that has been made. The yellow paint stops where it mixes with the grey and the two combine when you make the stroke. If the colour is correct then continue. Sometimes oils don't fix for days and you can loosen what you've done and blend in another shape. A small shape can make all the difference. There are no such things as rapid strides. Maybe with a pencil, yes — but with oils — the course is that of a heavy boat on a wild sea. Like a small boat — a barque that rises on the wave and falls on the other side. Always like a forward-looking barque.

Mornings were the natural time for Liska and me to paint. In the offices and industrial parks of Aberdeen, other men and women were forging through the tailgate of their labour. People were working outside in the yards, decks and warehouses of the harbour, and myself and Liska were in the studio — working too.

That is, if you call what we did *work*.

If you think we were just lazy — then I won't complain.

The fact is, that if you dream of the life of an artist, then it's up to you to pursue it. If your curriculum vitae is strong and you think you can get the proper investment — then why not be an artist? A couple of public commissions will guarantee your reputation, enough for you to apply for that grant you've always wanted. Travel to America, Italy, or Norway — it's really up to you.

> cf. Andy Warhol : *The Scream (after Munch)* (1985) pencil
> on paper, a very good copy indeed.

If you're working as a Parking Attendant you could be wasting your time. It is a common fact these days that one in three of the population is an artist — or should be an artist — and yet most of us insist on going to work because we claim we need to make the money. People just never get out of the cage and look at emancipation from the freedom side.

> cf. Fiona Rae : *Sky Shout* (1997) oil and acrylic on canvas.
> The artist clearly leading too liberating a life.

You don't need to cut yourself off from the world to be an artist. On the contrary, you'll have more time to go for coffee with the other artists.

Has the idea not already crossed your mind?

Have you not been dreaming Walter Pater in your toilet?

Have you not been thinking Joseph Beuys?

Why not join the Bowel Movement and get the ejectamenta on the flow?

Coprolite sponsorship awaits and your ordures have been delivered.

You needn't be a leading light, and you can do it in your lunch hour.

> cf. Amanda Heng : *Let's Walk* (1999) Woman drags a
> stool on a chain like a street lunatic. Passers-by pretend
> not to see. Lunch-hour art.

If Liska and I could get away with being artists for so many years then so could you. I wouldn't let anybody hold you back if you have the urge. You've only got the one chance and it's draining away right now. If you feel, however, that being a Parking Attendant is your calling, then that's good too. At least you won't have that dreadful modern feeling of having lost your soul.

I took a paintbrush over to Liska's corner of the flat — a paintbrush with a little yellow on the tip. Liska worked on the floor and not with an easel. The painting leaned against the wall and she crouched before it in her dungarees. I held the paintbrush and said: "Need any yellow?" and Liska turned. She smiled as if she had been stopped in the act of something wicked. Her cheeks put in an appearance and she said: "I've no idea what I'm doing!"

"Yeah you do," I said, and I painted the yellow on the doorframe.

Liska knew what she was doing, but if I caught her like this then her mind was a hundred miles north. I asked Liska if she wanted coffee — but she said no to that as well. From the kettle I watched her paint, and I wondered if painters could ever see their own work the way that others do. That was why painting was like becoming good at dreaming — that other counterfeit form of life.

I thought that the project Liska and I had decided upon — to complete our work as artists and then die — was the most successful attempt to challenge the art-world that I'd ever heard of. Ours was an effort with an earnest end point. We'd hardly sat down in the pub each evening before we began to talk again about the chances we would have by being dead. Which artists today consider death as a career move anymore? None, I think. I think they're probably accustomed to the high life, not on their expiry, but on their making that great leap to the auction room where the bidding increments leap 10% at a time.

12

■   We kept our paintings at our flat in Orchard Street. Slender iron pillars supported the outer ends of the steps and a wide pend opened into a basement stacked with Liska's supply of broken car windscreens, bus shelters, cinema hoardings and rusted iron spikes. Here, there was a darkly sufficient cellar where we kept our completed work, wrapped against the damp.

Anna Lunken brought a cheque for Liska one afternoon, a down-payment from Mr Sharma. She telephoned us from her jeep and arrived almost at the same time. She sighed from the bottom step and answered her mobile phone half way up the stairs. When Anna Lunken strolled across the doormat, her phone was still bleeping.

"I've brought you some dosh," she said. "I figure that you talented mothers (she swore here) need it more than we do!"

Anna Lunken held the cheque like a winning ticket and propped it on the window-sill. Cigarette smoke broke out of her face like a cone and she sat down on the sofa and said, "I hope it's enough."

Liska prepared tea in the kitchen and arrived with three cups.

"Are you going to take up Mr Sharma's offer?" asked Anna Lunken, but Liska managed to speak without offering a direct answer. Instead, she talked vaguely into her shirt of things coming to a natural point.

"Where are your paintings?" asked Anna Lunken.

She'd been glancing all over for our work since she had arrived.

"They're about," said Liska from the sanctum of her sofa.

"But where?" asked Anna Lunken.

"Part of finishing our work," said Liska, "is seeing if we can actually do that. I can't tell anybody where they are until they're done. I told you that my paintings are only to be seen as one."

Anna Lunken nodded like she understood. She knew that Liska

had destroyed the work that had been exhibited at the Myrtle Gallery and she didn't want to risk any more rash behaviour.

"I still wish you wouldn't destroy them," she said, but Liska was adamant in her rebuttal.

"You destroyed them when you saw them," she said.

Later, I walked Anna Lunken downstairs. We arrived at the dirty brown front door and I held it open for her.

"It's got to be clear," I said. "Liska wants her paintings to be seen but not sold. The money you gave us in no way represents the purchase of any work."

Anna Lunken tilted her head, ostrich-like.

"I'm leaving empty-handed aren't I?"

"You are," I said. "But all of this work stays together. You have to help us keep it that way. The same should apply to Mr Sharma and his studio."

I wasn't even registering on Anna Lunken's instruments.

"What's going on?" she asked.

Liska looked over the banister.

"What's going on?" she shouted.

"Nothing's going on!" I said.

Anna Lunken arrived at her jeep, and when she was inside and belted up, I waved.

"Bye!" I shouted — and when Anna Lunken looked at me, I smiled, because I was scared that she might realise that behind my teeth was a piece of gristle with her name on it.

Anna Lunken drove away at high speed and the grey matter of her exhaust fumes hung around longer than her memory. I stood in a daydream, staring at these gasoline-formed patterns in the air and enjoying the fact that their every movement was towards separation.

Upstairs, Liska was at work but I was through for the day. Anna Lunken or an empty tube of paint — anything to distract me. Some days all I needed was an excuse and I simply stopped working. Instead, I sat down at the window to drink myself once more into convincing myself that Liska and I should leave the world behind.

I stared at my hand and fell to thinking about what my next work of art would be. I thought about the Chinese artist Sheng Qi, who became famous in 1988 when he cut off his little finger in an exhilarating moment of romantic passion and idealism. It was just a finger one minute and then it was art the next — after he hacked it.

> cf. Sheng Qi : *My Left Hand in Blue* (2007) Acrylic on canvas, finger deceased.

That finger'll be out there somewhere, along with the top of Van Gogh's left ear and the missing toes of that creepy Russian guy, Nikolai Getman. Maybe the little finger is in a deep freeze and ready to make a surprise appearance or go on tour when he is due a retrospective — I don't know.

Staring at my hand, I realised that I'd happily exchange my little finger for Sheng Qi's level of fame — except that I couldn't do that, because that trick had already been pulled. I had a feeling that I was unlikely to succeed by painting alone however, which made me feel that I had to decide what I could sacrifice in order to make it in the art world.

Maybe how that's how death became the plan — because I couldn't think of anything else to cut off.

13

☐   Liska and I walked to the ferry terminal and we bought our tickets to the Shetland Islands with Mr Sharma's money. The staff at the terminal were angels, who handed over the tickets and told us to enjoy ourselves. We left the building and the ferry was parked right there, a huge blue steel contraption, topped with seagulls and sunlight.

"This is going to be so good," I said to Liska, and we held hands.

We walked slowly to the studio without talking, and when we got there we were surprised to see Joseph Gram drinking coffee with a handful of artists. Joseph Gram was so arch — he was smoking and wearing his usual black hat, and to see him there with the other artists you would have thought everyone had downed tools to hear Socrates.

When Joseph Gram saw Liska he stopped speaking. The way Gram held his arms out, so patronising I thought, I was happy to be leaving forever.

"We were just talking about you," said Joseph Gram.

The artists in the studio were excited that Gram was there, and he enjoyed the attention.

"Liska," said Gram. "I've been worshipping you from afar."

Gram smiled at me and called me a lucky man. He'd been in the middle of a speech, which he picked up again when he had our attention.

"There's a lack of contact between artists," said Gram, "that's why I've come here. I wanted to see where you all worked. It's come to me late but I know now what you're saying. There's no involvement in daily life. I see now that people want their art to be like everything else — just an adjournment from the business of the day to day. That's what we're talking about, isn't it?"

The others in the studio looked sheepish.

"Amazing," said Gram. "But I see that everything is an adjournment — and that there isn't anything in life that isn't adjourning all the time."

"I guess it's so," said Liska. "I hadn't thought of it like that."

"I look at what art has become," said Gram, "and I see that not only is there no direction but that we're forced into reproducing it faster in the hope that it might define itself. So that's why I think I need to start again. I feel the need to go back to a basic point, the point where art begins. I need to take my strategy from there — to try and inject some meaning into what I do."

It was classic Gram — narcissistic, and anchored in promise rather than action. I was sure that Gram had come to the studio to hang about with younger women — even to steal their ideas — but to my surprise, Liska agreed with him. When Liska talked, I noticed Gram listening closely and I wondered if he fancied her. Thoughts like that were spoiling everything, all the time.

Gram interrupted Liska and put his hand on her arm. "You were invited to Sharma's studio, weren't you?" he asked.

"Yes," said Liska, "but we can't do it."

Gram frowned. "We all need the money," he said. "It doesn't hurt to admit that."

"It's not that," said Liska, and she stared at her feet, her favourite ploy.

Gram looked puzzled. There was the hint of a smile beneath his supersaturated skin.

"We've got to go," said Liska. "We're working very hard at the moment."

"You've only just arrived," said Gram, and he twitched a cigarette into his mouth.

"We're going to Shetland!" said Liska, the closest she ever came to a suicide note, I realise.

A minute later Liska and I left Heery's studio, down the steps and back to town.

"What was that about?" I asked.

"It was about Joseph Gram," said Liska — and we crossed the street and joined the flow of pedestrians.

Seagulls followed closely and the stone blocks shone. We entered the nearest shopping centre with a sauntering walk of self-assurance. The shops were busy, as were the cafés, and even the recruitment offices were doing a little trade. The merely idle life of the artist was looking less than promising, as per usual.

"What are we doing?" I asked,

"I'll tell you what we're doing," said Liska. "We're going to pack up our work and then we're going to jump off the ferry — hand in hand."

"OK!" I said.

I felt less lonely, to be there with Liska. I even felt excited that we'd managed to elude responsibility as artists by famously not having sold anything at all. What comforted me the most was that Liska and I were together, the only ones who could make each other feel good about being in this world. Work was nearly done and nothing was in our way.

14

■ The truth of artists and their suicides is demonstrated by one of amateur psychiatry's most celebrated cases, Vincent Van Gogh. All of this is his fault for persuading the public that artists are mad and for arguing that special rules apply to them. As for the art, I'm not so sure. Art will continue in the future but in what form, it's difficult to say. What's not appreciated is that the artists are only ever the creators, and they don't define art, or the concepts that justify it. Art-lovers and art patrons bring the art world into being and the artists are always innocent.

> cf. Mario Molé : *L'art Pour L'art* (1956) One horizontal stucco picture frame with acanthus decoration. Nothing in the frame.

In the Middle Ages the painter's trade included tasks that would be considered menial by an artist today. On top of that, the very idea of anonymity is anathema to modern artists who need to be embedded in publicity in order to survive. Artists who are anonymous are considered poor and of low quality by those who decide upon these things — hence the new talent each year, and the fuss that goes with it. Hence the farting noise in the galleries — because whether traditional or concept, modern or antique, art is always the preserve of a certain public and not the popular domain it should be. One of the pioneers of this fashion was Joseph Beuys, who didn't make art for himself but was an expert at The Studio Game. Then there was also the lucrative tragedy of Diana Tropper, whose risqué pornography ran from studio to gallery, and gallery to studio, with no humanity in between. Ever since the industrial dawn increased our wall space we've bought up art as kudos. We've let it be known that art gives us that funny feeling inside and as a social bonus we like the status it gives us.

I've been an artist myself and have come to see the model for what it is, and to respond I can only follow Liska's rules. These are:

1. If you see anybody holding a glass of wine by the stem, run away.
2. If a silhouetted figure offers you money, this is probably the devil.
3. Remember that reason does overrule custom.

Given that most artists in the coming generations will be sponsored by corporations, it's safe to say that their attention will be drawn towards the Lunken Class.

> cf. Joseph Kosuth : *The object has taken the place of the ego ideal* (1989) white neon tubing sentence, 290cm long.

Artists will naturally object to the idea that they are working for anyone at all, but realistically they need to see where their money's from. It means that business professionals, multinational firms and other collectors are now art's arbiters, the very last people you would wish to see bringing home the good nature and truth that artists appear to peddle — but that's the state of things and that's why Liska and I needed to turn it round.

15

☐   Liska and I visited the suburbs and found Anna Lunken in her conservatory in a puffy green armchair. She was looking with a pained expression at a magazine. Anna Lunken stared for a long time at the advert on the back page and carefully shifted her weight before she put the magazine down. Liska and I stood in the tidiness of this house like unbrushed hair. It was something of a privilege to be asked there so that's why we turned up uninvited.

"You two," said Anna Lunken. "You look like a couple of tramps coming to collect."

"It's important," said Liska. "Our work is finished and we thought you'd better know."

"I've got a phone," said Anna Lunken, and she pointed to the pocket of her cream housecoat, from where poked the black plastic nub of her mobile communicator.

Liska stared. Her hands held her dress as if she was about to swing it in a dance, and she smiled and stamped her foot.

"You had to know!" she said.

Anna Lunken gave in and smiled. The magazine was discarded and her arms were folded in expectation.

"I need to see our contract," said Liska. "That's why we're here. I thought you'd have a copy. If something happens to us I want to see what we've agreed to."

"If something happens to you?" asked Anna Lunken, and she stared from the cold frame of her chair. Anna Lunken now had a strange feeling in her bones. "Do you not have a copy of the contract?" she asked.

If Anna Lunken had known Liska, she would have never have asked such a question. We took the Old Testament view about such covenants — they were sealed not by signatures but by eye contact and human agreement. A lawyer was not necessary in our view and if we ever wanted to see the paperwork we did the reasonable thing and requested it. To our knowledge, neither Liska nor I had been in the same room as a lawyer in our lives.

Liska waited for Anna Lunken to respond, the pads of her shoes tapping on the pine floor. Anna Lunken was looking to me for inspiration, any sort of hint as to what might be going on.

"We haven't got any of that stuff," I said. "It's not the sort of thing we keep handy. That's why we came here."

Anna Lunken straightened her trousers and I heard Liska say, "I knew this would happen."

"I'll get the file," said Anna Lunken, "but it's not going to do you a lot of good. There hasn't been any sale. I get the feeling that you're up to something. I dread to imagine what."

Anna Lunken walked more heavily than she had to. Her house coat was perfectly in tone with her surroundings, but the weight with which she thumped towards her study seemed unnecessary. Liska turned to me when Anna Lunken had left.

"I've got to be alone with the contracts," she whispered quickly. "Give me five minutes. Go into the garden with Anna Lunken. Distract her."

"What are you doing?" I asked.

Liska glanced into Anna Lunken's study where files were kept in yellow tin boxes, each one printed with its contents on the side. In the study, Anna Lunken browsed the nasty lemon files, running her finger down her life's work until she found the one she was looking for.

"Distract her," said Liska, "that's all."

Anna Lunken arrived and placed the metallic file down on her coffee table.

"Who wants something to drink?" she said. "Tea, coffee and all of the rest."

"Yes," I said, "let's make some tea."

I walked with Anna Lunken to the kitchen while Liska picked up the coloured tin box that held copies of our options and all the other fluff that Anna Lunken had collected.

"See you soon," Liska said, and she followed us to the kitchen door, which she closed behind us. Anna Lunken watched Liska through the glass and waved her fingers up and down. Liska took the file to the other side of the room and I left her to her plan, whatever it was going to be.

I was moved by the hygiene of Anna Lunken's kitchen and so I stared into the rubbish bin, which contrasted pleasantly with the prevailing tidiness. Perhaps somebody should look at all our rubbish, I thought. Before the mini mountain turns to milk and gum, before the rubbish goes down to the seaside archipelago, I thought. Each piece should be examined before it's forgotten about altogether. The jelly paste that's forming on the edge of town will be prehistoric butter one day — and someone should celebrate the fact that the rubbish'll keep returning to the blood cells of new-born people by an infusion of chemicals in our water.

> cf. Norman Guterman : *Winged Victory of Waste* (2004)
> Glass, wood, cardboard, cement, matt photographs of
> the artist's family.

Anna Lunken filled the strangest looking kettle I'd ever seen while outside a bird landed on the sill. Like the kitchen, Anna Lunken's garden was a pretty sight. Across several fields, a small passenger plane took off from the airport and nudged dramatically at the clouds.

"I hope I never lose Liska," Anna Lunken confided in me, and although I knew that the loss was inevitable, I nodded with unflinching frankness.

I figured that it was for time for me to invite Anna Lunken into the garden. I thought that if I could get her to talk me through a few of the flowers, it would pass time while Liska did what she was doing. When I opened the kitchen door though, Liska was already in action, running across the grass and climbing over the fence. Then Liska ran down the lane and away from Anna Lunken's house, towards the town. I noticed that Liska was carrying the yellow file in her arms. Liska's hair flew up and she was making the best speed possible.

"Oh, well," I thought. I saw the subtlety of the plan and it didn't matter what was going to happen next. This kind of approach was too direct for any good-minded person to fathom. It would be unlikely that Anna Lunken would even believe that it had happened.

Anna Lunken pulled three cups off a shelf and appeared behind me.

"Shit, this is pathetic," she said. "When we go back in I want the three of us to make a new deal."

"A new deal?" I asked as I blocked the door. I didn't want her to look over my shoulder and see Liska running down the lane.

"I know how you feel about selling your work," she said, "but I'm not like that at all."

Anna Lunken held a red cup, a yellow cup and a tartan cup. The kettle buzzed, indicating that it was time to progress to tea-leaves.

While Anna Lunken turned to the steaming pyramid that was the kettle, I had another look down the lane. Liska had reached the main road with the yellow box file.

"I'll take these through," said Anna Lunken, but I interrupted her.

"Whose is that sculpture in the garden?" I asked.

"Whose?" said Anna Lunken. "None, but mine."

It was a joke of sorts. Anna Lunken had chosen to ignore the artistic convention that on purchasing a work it remained linguistically at least, the property of the artist who had made it.

"Is it new?" I asked.

"Hardly," was her answer.

The tortured metal form that I had singled out was lurid, almost like an anchor gone wrong.

"It's going to rain," said Anna Lunken, and she disappeared to the living room.

When Anna Lunken came back to the kitchen she looked angry, as I expected. I was so nervous that I pretended not to hear her several times when she asked: "Where is she?" Eventually I asked Anna Lunken what she meant, but it was hardly a great acting performance. I walked through the house, pretending to look for my love in the bathroom, and shouting "Liska?" in a voice that wouldn't have persuaded a three-year-old that I was in earnest.

"This is ridiculous," said Anna Lunken.

"I'm sorry," I said. "I'll leave now and I'll be seeing you."

I left Anna Lunken's house and walked by a field of horses, down a line of beech trees to the main road. I passed granite houses and looked into the wide northern sky which carted away the sins of the nearby city. Less than two days were left before our trip to the islands and the final insight of the sea. I followed the river into town while dust blew across the traffic on the main road, and I remained in a dream right up until I reached our own front door.

16

■ Happiness and memory are, in the case of my love for Liska, one and the same thing. To remember in the present moment is to feel the possession of a joy. To be happy thereafter is to ignore the present questions of the mind.

Liska and I woke in the dark on our last morning and watched each other lain there. This was Liska's last day on earth and she looked upon it with a fearful sense of pleasure. We enjoyed a wine-led breakfast, both of us aware that shortly we were bound for the deep neck of the sea. This last mouthful of life was the easiest for Liska, and it was impossible that she should choke on it as she had on the millions of familiar actions of daily life. The recent past was annulled — the furniture of the art world was forgotten and our isolation had become a treasure. In those dark times, our final intentions were like a single lighted port in an ocean of night, and that was all we needed to survive.

"The two of us are inseparable," said Liska, "like two parts of the same cell."

Isolation, I found, fostered a strange fervour and a frantic zeal in me, perhaps due to the absence of an opposing voice or a contrary position. Isolation gave me the conviction of lucidity and sure sight. The inspiration isolation provides is certainly what dupes artists and like-minded god-seekers into their familiar ecstasy.

cf. Mandy Demand : *Nothing Reflects Nothing Reflects* (1999) Mirror, glass test tubes, pipe, dye.

As Liska and I departed for the ferry terminal these were the thoughts. We were breathless and bewildered. Liska had destroyed the contracts, and that was the last time we shall ever hear of them. We had no need to revisit the thoroughly mapped beginnings, middles and ends of our painting lives. We were ready to fit in another span in the bridge to a fuller understanding of the idea of the concept of the phenomenon that is known as art.

Our plan was to set sail for the Shetland Islands like any other passengers, but once we were far across the North Sea, we would jump from the ferry and participate in the highest form of ecstasy there is — a mutual end. Liska's pictures were wrapped and catalogued, mine too, for what they were worth. It was to be not just an expression of our bond, but an important artistic statement, a defiant act for young lovers such as we were then.

17

☐   Liska and I had in mind a gentle end in the sea, a drifting into sleep together, something more romantic, we believed, than killing ourselves, or whatever other derogatory terms are used for what we'd planned. From the deck of the ferry, Liska admired the ornament in the waters, where patches of foam turned and bubbles trowelled up from where colours were at their hardest to define. From the North Sea, our old hometown of Aberdeen was a dreamland on the coast, lighting up for the evening.

> cf. Lawrence Weiner : *A Sound Grown Softer (diminuendo)* (1971) Writing on wall, variable dimensions. The making of a work, the passage from the verbal-conceptual to material form, is not a necessity, only an option of equal status.

Everything at speed. We could have been the happiest people in the world, standing at the bow of the ship in the perfect nonplus of our drunkenness. We looked down into the swell of water and I thought that perhaps we might forget ourselves and die peacefully on deck.

I became dizzy as we opened the sea-door to the lounge. The bar was lined with drinkers whose speech I could hear above the turning of newspaper pages. Their mutter rose from the same soul-sucking northern argots I'd heard all of my days, and everywhere you went in that room, was the feeling that somebody nearby had just been sick.

"I'm ready now," I said. "Let's have our last lesson at the bar."

Liska and I walked through the sick-lounge and ordered two glasses of vodka and tonic — and during those minutes I heard nothing but the whirr and roar of the boat's engines clashing with our plans. We knocked glasses and the vodka shot down. Liska asked for another two and pushed her glass along the bar.

"You haven't paid for those two yet," said the man who was serving.

Everything at speed, I thought, and I smiled at him roundly.

Liska plonked her money on the bar and began to count it out on a cloth.

"Come on," I said to Liska, and we drank again, no more slowly.

"This is awful stuff," said Liska.

I'd been worried about our last moments for a long time. Even at that late hour I was waiting for life to consume me, so that I wouldn't have to do it for myself. I was meditating so hard on the clock behind the bar that I felt dead just by looking away from it. Time had worked for a while, life had worked for a time, but in the bar of the boat, mortality clicked round faster than was normal.

"Some more," said Liska. "You don't want to feel it do you?"

This was far too demanding a question, and muscle and hope twitched at the same time in my sour stomach. Liska had the right idea. She was looking forward to the surprise of the cold water — either that or she was just laughing at the joke.

"There's not long to go," she said, and I thought of her and me in our sweet rest far away.

Our plan was to jump from the boat — we'd made our decision and were acting on it. I was sure that it had been my idea. Under the covers of the bed I'd thought about the pill bottle but then turned my mind to floating in the sea. Bed is the customary space for thinking about the end of life and later, when daylight comes and people's voices rise from beneath the window, these foolish ideas evaporate. Hence, thoughts of self-murder only came like witches in the night. We'd talked about it for a year and we were ready.

The drink was turning to vapour in my stomach and it relaxed my spine, which was bent into a letter C on the barstool. Liska was ordering another one, another two, and one for the barman. In the mirror behind the bar, I was reduced to a foggy face with a drink. Suddenly the unsolvable character in the mirror became of interest to me.

"Move up," said a guy who nudged in beside us for no reason. This guy had no hair and wore a storm-jacket.

"You," I said to him.

The storm-jacket guy didn't have the first idea what it meant, but it made him laugh.

"You! Me!" he said

"That's right," I said.

This storm-jacket man took a hold of me and tried to lift me along the counter so he could have more space.

"Business or pleasure?" he asked, still nudging with the oversized elbow.

The matter was past dispute.

"It has to be business," said Liska.

"I've been to the islands fourteen times," said the storm-jacket man. He looked directly past me and into the centre of Liska's dress. I was now officially no longer there.

"You've got relatives on the islands?" asked Liska.

"Girlfriends," he said.

A shiver ran through my vodka belly. It was all lies. Listening to the cowardly trifles of this passenger, who wouldn't want to drown?

Liska laughed and said "Girlfriends!" and he laughed too.

"Yeah," he said, "I've Fiona and Lorna. I've shagged Fiona's mum too but now I only see Fiona when she gets down to the hotel."

It was the most banal moment of my life. The storm-jacket man turned to me with the creative power of a dream and winked. I was appalled and yet I smiled. Liska smiled too. It happens that you meet a guy who boasts his sexual conquests and normally sane women seem to think that it's all right. Liska might have been laughing at him, but I felt like a coward for not pushing him off his stool.

"Rain or shine," he said, "Fiona's always there!"

"How did you meet Lorna?" asked Liska.

I sighed, but neither Liska nor storm-jacket seemed to bother.

"I met her on this very boat," he said. "She was over there with her daft friends and I bought her a drink. We got pissed but you know the thing. When we got off the boat I took her number."

Liska was grinning as if interested — it was an odd smile, like something a drunk had discarded and she'd picked up and worn.

"We're pretty close, Lorna and me," said storm-jacket. "She says that she looks forward to my visits so I can't complain can I?"

Liska and I said no in unison. I'd suffered enough but I could still be polite.

"It's Fiona that's got it made for me though," he said. "She can hardly get enough, ken?"

"It's beautiful," said Liska — she spoke in a voice displaced. I tapped my fingers, but both she and the storm-jacket guy ignored my impatience.

"Drink up," said the guy, and Liska turned and asked the barman to do us all more drinks. Our money was still on the bar and I counted it. I had no intention of spending my last few hours watching the storm-jacket guy chatting up Liska. I felt a desire to recollect, to reconsider memories from our shapeless past.

But look. Drink had changed everything and retrospection met a brick wall. There was nothing here to recall that wasn't lost already. In theory everyone looked wonderful. Everybody was at the end of his or her life and not just me. All those wives and workers, husbands and travellers drinking in the distant and millennial kingdom of the floating bar — it was like a trip to the moon. The boat croaked up and down, the sky was black, and people sat in circles in the promise of each others' company. It was nothing special and yet something I'd never managed to grasp. Soon I would be drowning. None of the people there would ever know what had happened. They had lives of their own that I couldn't explain, and there seemed to be so much more to tell.

"You'd be better to hide that money," said the storm-jacket guy.

He pointed a ringed finger at the cash we'd spread on the bar top. "Who knows, you might need it tomorrow."

This statement surprised Liska.

"What is it?" he said.

I saw myself as he might see me. All I did was sit like a dope and wonder what the consequences of my next action would be.

"I'd like to get all the rapists and punish them," said Liska. "That's what'll happen when I'm God."

"What?" asked the guy. He shook his head.

"Look at it like this," she said. "The amount of people who've got away with it — what about them? There'll be no consolation and worse, there'll be no remorse. Life'll just go on. No retribution either. That's why when I'm God, it'll all change — and that's why it'll be the first thing to change."

Liska drank her vodka in silence — the storm-jacket guy wasn't sure what she might have been suggesting. I sensed that a structure was about to be knocked down. The guy said nothing, his cheeks seemed particularly vulnerable.

"It's an old idea," said Liska. "Capture hundreds of slaves, kill the men and rape the women. Now multiply that by several centuries. This is what they used to do to women, isn't it?"

"I agree," said the guy. He looked at me as if I'd some part to play in this. It wasn't the case though. I had been dreaming and not concentrating.

"I think what to do," said Liska, "is get all the rapists into one town. When I'm God, it'll be easy. The thing with some people is that you can never make them see their crime. Even if they acknowledge their guilt, which they don't, I can't rape every rapist can I? No, I can't do that. So that's a problem."

Liska ordered three more drinks though the storm-jacket guy had barely touched his.

"So," said Liska, "what to do with the rapists? You've got all these butch psychopaths who are ruining everything. I mean, for all we know we could all be descended from them. What if that's true? It probably is true because you can't be selective about your genes. What if you've got the same genes as one of those rapists?"

The storm-jacket guy hadn't moved. "So what?" he said.

Liska gave the storm-jacket guy his drink and slid mine to the area of the bar where I had thrown my money. Her eyes blazed like a house on fire.

"When I'm God," she said, "we'll undo the pain. That's the only way it can work. First the violence will be a memory but ultimately it won't exist. I mean, look at you. I bet you like a lot of violence."

"Violence?" said the storm-jacket guy.

Liska's sentences were becoming more conclusive.

"Well, think of it as sex," she said.

Our drinking companion was not able to make the association that Liska had made between sex and violence, and Liska looked like she was restraining the desire to laugh.

"For crying out loud," she said — and she rested her hand on the guy's arm — maybe an act of pity. "What I'm saying is that we'll just make sure that violence is taken out of memory altogether, and then because violence won't exist — and cannot exist — then it never will have existed. You see what it's going to be like? If one sort of violence stays, then all violence will be permitted — although to remove it all is not outwith our powers. Certainly not beyond the powers of God."

"I'm going for a shit," said the guy, "what do you think of that?"

He slipped off the barstool and looked at us both. Liska stared with a farsightedness that reminded me why I loved her.

"Don't worry," said Liska. "The world will ignore you and you'll be forgotten. All violence will be forgotten."

"That's bullshit," said the guy.

He swigged his drink and smiled falsely.

"The world's already turned its back on you," said Liska.

"You're crazy," said the guy, and he wiped his lip.

Our friend didn't see this as a threat, but, given that I was about to throw myself into the sea, I found the idea a horror. Not to exist meant not to have ever existed — and that meant there would be no memory of me at all.

The storm-jacket guy went below to relieve the tension of Liska's attack, but I wished that he'd stayed with us now. I loved Liska when she got started because she genuinely had no rules.

The guy chanced another lustful look at Liska before he left the bar. We watched his big bum shove towards its promised end and I felt truly drunk. I would have stayed like that forever, high as hell and at the point of sickness — but it was time to go. I watched the storm-jacket guy leave the bar and I felt awful for Fiona and Lorna. Those dark islands, with their flat grass banks and oil sumps in the ocean. They were all going down with us into the sea.

Click here to abort this world and start again.

We drank up and Liska sorted through her money. The more we drank, the more coins she seemed to collect.

"Have we left the harbour yet?" she asked.

"Two hours ago," said the man behind the bar.

"We'll have a couple more," she said. "Then we'll have one to go."

18

■ This wasn't what I'd expected of our evening at sea. I'd imagined Liska and myself cuddling at the bow and saying our prayers at the critical point of departure — now a doubt blazed up within me. It was true that our first love had transformed into something else, a commitment to our final pact. We met and joined like two parts of the same cell, she said — and once we were joined like that, it was difficult for anybody else to be admitted. We'd sent our keys to Heery the Hippie of Multiple Solitude, and walked from Orchard Street to the ferry terminal. Liska had left her paints and a cassette player. I had left my paints, notebooks, an antique lamp, my bedding and two filing cabinets, plus a multitude of other disposable crap.

Liska and I drank the last drinks fast — and the last drinks after that arrived. By this time I would say the barman knew that we had planned an early night.

"You two," he said, "should watch out."

I looked at Liska and, reassuringly, I didn't know her. Once you embark on such a project it's difficult to know when to say goodbye and I realised that we'd already said it. Liska looked around the bar and I had the feeling she wanted to speak to someone else. Instead she looked at the barman again.

"You seem like a happy guy," she said to him.

"Yes," he replied.

He put his hands on the counter to listen to what Liska had to say. I swayed on my stool. I was thinking of all the people who had died in the way we were planning to, and how sad it would be to die unwanted. The barman had fixed us both with a gaze, essentially of love — the barman's gaze of love, for those about to drink and die. A barman is a barman the whole world over, I thought. Even in the North Sea, a barman is just the same and dispenses the same long gaze when you're not looking.

> cf. Chinese Northern Wei Dynasty : *Standing Buddha* (AD 447) Gilt Bronze. Seems to be welcoming worshippers.

Liska and I held hands when we left the bar. The carpet tilted slightly because we were already ghosts. Cold air swirled around the fruit machines and we walked towards the rear of the ship. I could have had a heart attack right there. The sweat on my hands reminded me of the summer that Liska and I met. Neither of us could balance but we managed a deathly dignity as we walked the aisles of seats, where the ship's recliners gave us half an eye.

Our walk through the ship was a judgement at each step. A child passed with a toy and I wanted to ask him if he knew us. The ship was dark at the rear, the door to the deck was heavy. I looked at the child again and then I was outside, looking over the sea, which was blacker than I could ever have imagined it.

The waters were like moving rock, flowing unconsciously away. Liska was ahead of me and I let the door close.

There were two other people on deck as we arrived at the stern and we took some steps to where there was a platform. Still dreaming, I held the handrail and wondered why I was scared of slipping. The platform was wet, and as the grey ice of the night hit my nostrils, I became aware of the cold. The sound of the sea was like the noise of space, breathless and loud and coming from all sides.

> cf. Wyndham Lewis : *What The Sea is Like at Night* (1949) Pen and ink, watercolour, gouache, pencil, charcoal and coloured chalk. A vortex like no other.

I climbed on the rail and Liska got up beside me and placed one leg over. We could barely look at each other, we were both so fixed on the surface of the sea, with its swirling patches of black. The sight of the waves was enough to make me gasp for air and my body felt like a piece of mould about to be wiped away. Tiny leaves of white broke from the water and vanished in the noise. The farewell tears began and I tried to avoid the blackness of the night. Instead I looked into the sleeve of Liska's jacket, while the spray from the sea rose like a trail of clouds.

I never did like that jacket of Liska's, I thought — although I seemed to think that I loved it then.

I opened my eyes at some point — maybe when somebody took my wrist. Then I pretended to fall, as if I were about to fall, even though the arms that held me were firm. The arms that held me knew how to act and they had anticipated me in every way. All waters, all grottoes of water, all waves, all fools and all bodies — the recurring event was of a fall that was not happening — and Liska had gone ahead of me, down into the sea.

19

☐ I have the type of memory that is largely useless as a way of lending order to the recounting of experience. Most of what I recall is so implausibly textured with fantasy that I sometimes think that all of it has been invented. These are the sweets of love, which rewrote everything. The pointing of the writing that survives in the hand of love is very light indeed.

I recall that first date with Liska, when we ran away to sleep beside the golf course for a night. The incidence of myself and Liska meeting and the summer we spent together, these are the repeated items of memory that have shaped my thinking. When daylight forms above the North Sea each morning there's a patch of blue that waits for longer than the night. This is an exceptional blue, an established point in the sky that rises with the morning. That dawn, we sat on the rocks at St Catherine's Dub in a growth of aquatic grass, and we talked about that blue place. After that, we drank more wine and talked about our dreams — and I held Liska's hand. Liska was occupied with the nest of her desires in a cut diamond bed on the grass floor.

"Why can't we have a shrinking economy instead of one that grows?" she asked.

Legs of weed flowed out of the bank and the rocks jutted up in order.

I grabbed a stalk of grass and pulled.

"We could have an economy where zero was the highest you could pay for anything," she said.

I could see it.

"You'd be given everything for free, then?"

"Not necessarily," said Liska, "but it would be more efficient than the economy that we've got. Each year they'd say how much money had been taken out of the world and everybody's resources would be deflated accordingly. Investments would reduce and owners would offer their tenants a share of the property to decrease their profit."

The idea bore witness to the murderous proclivities of our own landlords.

"How about it then?" asked Liska.

"You'd have to make the cheapest things the most expensive," I said.

Liska sat in a nook of grass and looked to where an abandoned log lay like an arm stretching into the sky. "If everything was in reverse," she said, "then you'd only do a job that you wanted to because you'd be paying to do it."

"Lots of jobs would disappear."

"For sure. It would mean that there'd only be a tenth left to do that there is now."

"A twentieth."

"More," she said. "And more services would be done for free because people wouldn't accept money for them."

"So in this economy everything's deflating towards zero?"

"Yes — all the time. There'd be no interest and no need for profit. Anybody who made anything would be paying for the fact that they did so."

"That's too much," I said.

"You can't draw the line now," said Liska. "You've agreed so far, so you've got to go all the way. Your savings are going to become lower each year — so think how immeasurably low they can get. You could almost reach zero if you decide to buy nothing at all."

"Well I don't know."

"What don't you know?"

Liska had figured out the path to nothingness.

"Don't lose your confidence," she said. "Remember that as long as people are going to need more money instead of less, the majority of them are going to do anything to get it."

Liska was right about that. Life could be a matter of sticking to your convictions — it's harder than you might think.

"Would it solve the problems of the world?" I asked.

Liska and I left that sandy cove, up a path of summer brambles, the type that tug on your clothes.

"The problems of the world are mirrors of the minds that dreamed them up," said Liska. "Some of the problems are so developed that they're claiming hundreds of lives every hour. Some of these same problems are the work of political systems — and several of them are being discussed right now by the parties that you voted for. Sad, but all the parties call for the same cure-all — money."

Liska took my hand and I began to wonder why we had so little money.

"Money is the medicine," she said, "and when we can't resist the tragedies of the world any longer, more of it is what is always asked for."

"More Money!"

What do the arts need? More money! What do the hospitals need? More money! What do the poor need? More money! A strange and unhappy conclusion — when in fact all of the problems of the world, as Liska said, were dreamed up in our own minds.

Liska fell over and laughed at the idea of a world with no money. She smiled from the grass and I watched her with the thoughtful assurance that, alive or dead, everything was going to be all right.

20

■   Something was coming to an end. The brief pleasure of enlightenment had passed and I was less wise than before. I couldn't pinpoint the final reason I wanted to jump from the ferry into the sea but only Liska had managed to do it. It appeared that in her death, as in her life, Liska's honesty concerning her intentions had been indubitable — unlike mine. Surely I didn't want to drown only to increase the value of my artwork?

Liska lay in the crib of the sea and the Sailing Captain tannoyed the ferry to say that there had been an accident. The sun rose jestingly from the water as the ferry arrived in Shetland and sailed between the locks of land on which the houses appeared like oddly spaced stones. Cramped at the back of the bay was the town of Lerwick, and from the jetty people were staring at the boat like they hated me already.

The police force took their foothold and were on deck, standing before me, staring from under their tarmacadam hats. The Sailing Captain spoke to the police for five minutes because nothing that I'd related about Liska's disappearance had been clear. All evidence turned on the words of one holiday-maker who had seen us both leaning over the side.

"They two'd been in the bar," said the Sailing Captain to the police officers.

One of the cops opened his notebook for my name. The occasion of my suicide had passed in failure and the period of explanation had begun. The policeman's notebook filled:

> Guy Poynting
> Liska, seems to have forgot her second name. Shock?
> Brown hair.

Blue trainers blue trousers green cardigan t-shirt
reading shoplifters of the world unite black jacket says
he lost it in the bar
6.30 pm ferry to Lerwick
Green eyes / girl drowned from back of ferry
Both leaning over the side DRUNK witness 10.30pm
No body / impossible location / artist called Liska —

"Are you sure you can't remember her surname?" asked the cop.

Ahead of me, the town of Lerwick shrugged out of the dark. There were more police on the quayside and an ambulance had pulled up. The night's passengers sidled away with heavy bags. Day should never come, I thought. Day means light and light means truth.

One of the policemen drew the Sailing Captain aside and there was a conversation. Again, I heard the key phrase: both leaning over the side. There was more to come and I waited in paralysis.

The image ran through my mind's eye. Liska flew away. She seemed to go up rather than down. The truth of my cowardice seemed too intolerable and to talk or think much about what had happened would have been an admission of the fact that I'd let Liska die alone. I wondered what the police could charge me with for that? Shoulder-shrugging self-preservation, presumably. Mortus interruptus. Another police car slid along the quay to the small party near the gate of the dock. The policeman near me gave me no clue as to what might happen next.

At the police station I was asked more questions concerning the logistics of my misadventure. The holding room was an old brown cell for people who weren't criminals yet, but still had no right to a cushion. The policeman's voice was like a broken tambourine, and yet I could still make out his words. The police wanted to know if Liska had jumped from the boat or if she had fallen — or if she had slipped — or if there were drugs involved — or if I felt that alcohol had been a contributing factor. We had been seen acting in a drunken fashion on the boat that evening, as several local drunks had testified.

"Liska," he said, "was that her name?"

I nodded. Everything was so reasonable and I could hide my motives indefinitely.

"Why did you have her ticket in your pocket?" he asked, but there was no answer to this question.

"Do you think she killed herself?"

"Did you intend to kill yourself?"

"I was trying to talk her out of it," I said, and this was written down.

I had told my first lie and it had been so painless that I told some more. Subsequent lies drifted so far from reality that the mood of the interview room soon became one of sympathy for my cause.

"I was trying to talk her out of it," I said.

"Was she on the boat for that?"

"We didn't have anything planned," I said.

"You were on holiday?"

"We were artists," I said.

A procession of three officers left the room, leaving me with a bladder-faced cop in a low hat who put his hands behind his back. I was tired and so I tried to rest, but when I closed my eyes I imagined Liska hitting the water again. First the body broke the surface and then it tore through as if breaking into a different realm. There was a crash from down the corridor and a laugh. I opened my eyes to a sympathetic glance from my guard and I put my head on my arms and waited for the next episode.

cf. Sarah Lucas : *Human Toilet* (1997) C-print 96 x 74 inches. £15,000 to see Sarah on the pan.

I was never going to be assured of a place on the stage as an actor. All I could manage to be was scenery, which meant that all I had to do was wait in order to be shifted. One lie would lead to another and it was all being recorded. I suspected the police knew my real motive for not jumping, so I turned my lies over in my mind in the hope that they'd stay fresh enough for me to snake through any remaining questions.

Eventually they led me from the interview room to a nicer area which offered magazines and newspapers. I tried to remember why I had wanted to jump, but I couldn't. I stared at the newspaper instead. The repetition and randomness of the letters confused me. There was writing in those messages, symbols prompting engagement with the printed words — but what did these words mean? I read the words in the Aberdeen daily paper but nothing was clear in any of the headlines, which included:

CHURCH DEPLORES GAY DECISION
NO SYMPATHY FOR FAKE ARSENIC CLAIM
FARMERS ACCUSED OF SECRECY

The next police interview amounted to the same questions and lies, all recorded for the authorities.

"Do you have any friends or relatives in Shetland?" asked a policewoman who had been appointed for sympathetic reasons. This copper's ears were like barn doors and supported spectacles like windows to an aquarium. Something in her big face suggested a viciousness that put the fear of lying in me.

"I used to have friends here," I said.

The policewoman thought about writing this down but instead she tapped her pen and stared at me. "They used to be your friends or they used to stay here?"

"Both," I said.

The interviewing cop scratched a barn door and wrote this down.

I was escorted to the front desk by the same guys who had picked me up. They took my arm as if I couldn't manage the corridor without veering into the wall. I was another piece of gum on the shoe of the world, another casualty in the failure of man. There were more forms to fill and the Maitre d' Cop at the front desk told me that I'd be heading back to the mainland by aeroplane.

"I've never flown on a plane before," I said, but the cop wasn't impressed.

"Time you will fly now," he said, and he opened a file. "Put your address here," he said, and his finger drew across the form to the obvious box.

I was playing a part but couldn't help myself. I couldn't help my weak knees and the falling over. As I tried to walk to a seat, a policeman caught me. The door of the waiting room was open and two ladies in the waiting area saw me being manhandled into a seated position. I slipped off the seat and I was in the officer's arms again. I glanced to see the two ladies looking on with interest, both of them cradling their shopping. I dragged myself up the chair and asked for water.

"I want to die," I said, and I think a part of me did die. Certainly the room became dark — either that or my head clouded so badly that I may as well have been in a dream. Consciousness was hard to keep a hold of, I found. One minute I was there and the next I was in the dreamless beyond. It was to be a pattern that repeated as I got to grips with grief.

"How can you say that you want to be dead?" asked the dream-cop.

"I don't know," I told him, "but sometimes it seems so obvious, and necessary."

This policeman's moustache frightened me, and so did his stick. He didn't need the stick but there it was in his belt. "You think you're so clever," he said, "but I hear this rubbish all the time. People say that voices tell them to commit crimes. So many criminals and they're all in a daze and hearing voices."

"Part of me wanted to go," I said, and I looked down the corridor to the exit. "I really wanted to jump but I couldn't."

The police bore down on me with his stock expression. "Look," he said. "You can't just split your actions into percentage chances and then judge what you were doing on that basis, like. If you say that part of you wants one thing but another part of you wants something else, then you're lying, ken? You're not made of parts sonny. You're made of one body that either does or doesnae. Don't give yourself airs in here."

"But I've got conflicting voices," I said.

The policeman slammed his stick down on the plastic chair and the thud made me jump out of my wits. The chair had cracked in half and the black stick was raised to the moustache level of the policeman holding it.

"Next time that's your head," he said. "Now try and think about what you're saying. This luxury of yours. The many voices that you hear. This wee gang in your skull that tells you your decisions before you announce that you can't make up your mind. What's that to the rest of us?"

The noise of the stick smashing on the chair again.

"I just can't work this out," I said to the policeman.

The cop moved his stick behind his head, as if to scratch his neck. "Which of your voices is speaking now?" he asked.

The cop wasn't trying to be funny, he was merely asking a sensible question of a person having a bad dream.

"I don't know," I said, "somebody's confusing me."

"You know where the sea is," said the policeman. "You can jump into it any time you like. It's a bloodless death. Violent, yes, but no blood. I see that as a mark of purity, ken? The sea really does swallow them down, not like a car crash or jumping from a bridge. I appreciate that. Less work for us."

{*Silence fell and the lights rose. I opened my eyes.*}

The policeman at the desk was completing a form of many pages. "You need to sign here," he said, and he managed a touched expression. "The search will be called off shortly. You must understand. We don't even know where to look."

I signed the final form and was led away. Outside, the small island town of Lerwick had converted from an early morning dungeon to a brisk turn of vehicles and people. A police car waited to take me to the airport and I shuffled into the rear seats. The driver let off the clutch and we puttered up the brae with my head beating bass-drums, full of fear for the coming days.

21

☐   Our civilisation is not mystically inclined, although the head-on collision between Religious Antiquity and Enlightened Hysteria has resulted in such a Botched Modernity that one would be foolish not to find the place a delight. In this Fluid Conceptuality, the aeroplane that raised me from the Shetland Islands could be interpreted as the functional equivalent of my saintly passport to the clouds.

Flying was just like I thought it was going to be — an absurdity above all others. The passengers seemed jaded, like they'd had too much of a good thing, and in contradiction to this, I felt quite well, being the only person there who wanted the aeroplane to crash.

An air steward approached and the passengers unfolded newspapers in cramped positions, each to their own tent of news. I could see every front page but there had been no air disasters that day.

> cf. Cornelia Parker : *Hat Burned by a Meteorite* (2000)
> burned tweed hat (7.5 x 28 x 29.1 cm) This work is
> accompanied by a certificate of authentication signed
> by the artist. It's the certificate which distinguishes
> this burned hat from any other burned hat.

My thoughts turned faster than I could deal with them. I heard Liska's name or maybe I had spoken it to myself in half-sleep. Don't tell me, but I was thinking about that burned hat, it sold for so much money. I was using the hat to black out other thoughts, but that sort of approach can only drive you mad. It's not the burned hat itself that offers value, I thought. Nothing has intrinsic value. I wonder if Liska died instantly?

I realised that Liska may have spent some time in the water before she died, and I closed my eyes, under the impression that denial may make the question go away.

Maybe it had been three minutes and maybe it had been thirty.

How would I know?

How could anyone say with any accuracy what goes on in the North Sea?

All I can say is that assuming Liska didn't die on hitting the water, she would have known for some time what was going to happen. Further, she would have been able to watch her salvation recede. I returned to Aberdeen with these thoughts in mind and no way to stamp them out.

Everything from necessity, however. There needs to be at least one burned hat artwork in the world. And I had to hope that it had been quick for Liska, though I don't know why I doubted it.

On landing, I was released from the aeroplane and I headed for the area of the city that we used to call our home, Orchard Street. In the flat I wondered what to do without Liska. It was late in the afternoon and tapers of sickness trailed up my throat, and light bounded off everything that we'd kept and treasured. I was there with all our paintings, standing inside the memory itself, but now Liska was gone and I was alone to work it out.

22

■ Just as I vomited in the lavabo of our home — even then I realised that the rent was due. Our possessions were packed in fruit boxes and I noticed that the dishes were clean for the first time and the bins had been emptied. Liska's work was wrapped in tanned paper, stacked at the window. My pictures were fewer than Liska's and were packed in the spare room. Beside our pictures were our notebooks, our makeshift gifts to posterity.

The work of two artists who came back from the dead?

It could be.

> cf. René Magritte : *The Cubiste Coffin* (1944) Signed 'Magritte' lower right. Sealed oak coffin containing all aesthetic and moral concerns.

For a moment I dallied among the notebooks before I fell asleep amid an ingress of unwelcome thoughts. I lay on the rug until there was a banging on the door, which woke me again. The noise was like the crash of the sea and I pulled the rug around me and remembered where I was. I was in the flat and there was a filthy rapping coming from the landing and I couldn't move for fear of pain.

When the knocking stopped, I curled into the rug in the immovable peevishness of a sulk, and when a quiet hour had passed, I rose and exited to Orchard Street. I walked the darkest way round to the night garage where I read a newspaper until I found what I was looking for. Liska was in the paper with the politics and the world affairs, there in her own text-boxed coffin. Mist rolled along Orchard Street, threatening the coastal streets and quarters of Aberdeen, but not able to make it up to the town. I sat on a wall for several minutes and watched a large car roll by, its lights dipped low.

Back in the flat I spread the paper on the table. My eye yielded reluctantly to the photograph of Liska, the very first time her photograph had been in a newspaper. Liska looked up at me from the table. I had told her that I was going to jump into the sea with her and float to the happy place at the bottom — but in fact I froze — for whatever reason she did not know. In spite of the anvils clanging in my head I read the article several times, and even though facts were few, the one or two the writer had managed to collect were largely wrong.

I sat on the edge of the chair, knees tight-closed, withdrawn as I thought things through. It wasn't until I saw the dawn creep at the edge of the tattered curtains that I began to wonder if I hadn't wanted to outlive Liska and see what the world would be like without her. It was a limbo which I'd craved ever since we'd talked about dying, as close a place to the living end as may be found. All that whimwham, and all that blether, I hadn't meant it ever.

Did Liska do everything that she wanted to before she died?

Did Liska still close her eyes when she danced?

I lowered myself to the couch to sleep and while I dropped off, I invited in another thought — the idea that I had killed Liska and that I was nothing short of a murderer.

I wondered if Liska could still be floating in the sea and waiting to die with the chill running up her legs. She could still be falling off the back of the boat, I thought — I didn't know how it worked. I imagined Liska's life flashing before her eyes as she fell, a long showing — even for a flash. I wondered if Liska could still be watching hers. If you were watching your life flash before your eyes, what would happen when you reached the point in your life, when your life flashed before your eyes?

23

☐ The knocking continued the following morning, and I reached the door hoping that it would be somebody with drink, or at least coffee, but it was Heery the Hippie of Multiple Solitude. Heery had nothing with him but a shocked expression. My hair snapped back and Heery took my arm without being able to define the level of my invalidity.

"We're not going to talk about it, man," he said. "But we are going to take you out of here."

A short involuntary impulse, and I coughed.

Heery gripped me. "Have you been in here all this time?" he said.

"I don't know," I replied.

Heery guided me to our short sofa. I glanced in the mirror and I did not look well, clearly an unstable element, settled on a catalyst.

"Frau Lunken's been looking for you," said Heery. "She wants to know what's happened. She wants to know if you're all right."

It was late in the morning and the hour hand of our clock had made an entire sweep in the night. Heery stood at the kitchen door against the splendid background of our yellow mural.

"Anything you want?" he said.

Heery looked quaintly human. It was only two days since I had been at sea with Liska — two days since she'd washed cold to the bottom. I saw her floating on her back, head-first and cast away, dropping into the planet in a long dress like a ghost diver. I saw myself weary and dreamy, as if lost in a vast open space.

"What are you mumbling?" asked Heery.

My tongue rolled out the clicks of some words and the sound kept my thoughts from the subject of Liska with remarkable effect. I got to my feet and said: "The pictures."

"We'll get them," said Heery, and he flung my old jacket from the chair.

My neck was sore and tears had dried across my eyes. It was like not being able to see properly, which was appropriate for grief. I stood on the landing like a child who didn't want to leave the house, a little too tall for the role I was playing. I gurgled — I was saying something about the flat but I was still essentially wordless.

Heery said to me, "It doesn't matter," and I knew that it did not.

"Last time I left here I didn't think I'd be coming back," I confessed and Heery led me gently on. We reached the bottom of the stairs and the hall woke me with its strangeness. I wondered if I was really suffering grief or whether it was guilt. I gripped Heery's coat as we arrived in the broad day.

"What am I going to do?" I said.

I was as helpless as I'd ever been — I was supposed to be dead after all. I was intended for the sea but I'd escaped like an undissolved pill that was going back into the bottle. I felt brave that I'd even hung off the back of the boat.

"We're going to my place," said Heery. "It'll be good." Heery looked me in the face and his kindness dazzled me for a second. "Is there anything you want from upstairs?" he asked.

I looked at Heery and felt hopelessly mad. "No," I said, and I walked beside him up the street.

Remembering the glorious happiness Liska and I had shared as artists, I started to breathe more freely. I recalled how, fired by each other, Liska and I had made our world-ending decision as only lovers could. In our old house the curtains were drawn and Liska's paintings were still in there. I had the only key to the house and so I stopped and crouched for a minute, gripping it in my hand, pretending to tie my shoelace.

Heery stopped too — and one second later, the silent street was broken by the clatter and plop as I pitched our house key down the nearest drain and, with no further thought, I rose and continued up the hill.

There was just one other thing, but at the top of our road, something odd happened that seemed perfectly appropriate — a parking attendant stopped and raised his hat to me.

Death, you discover, is one cliché after another, and yet that old-fashioned idea of removing your hat from respect was one I was not expecting — certainly not from one of the city's car parking wardens.

"Do I know you?" I asked, but he shook his head — and with that Heery and I continued undisturbed across the town.

24

■ At Heery's house in Torry I was impatient to get under the covers. There were a few people there, including artists from the studio and a couple of their anarchist friends. They were drinking beer and looked guilt-ridden that they might be enjoying themselves in the presence of such a ghost as I.

"We're sorry," they said, and I looked down. The anarchists even looked sorry too, not a pretty sight. I wondered how they would behave if they knew that I'd let Liska go? Everybody was aware there was something they didn't know, which made this worse.

"You've got a nice view of the harbour," I said, looking from the pearly grey gable of Heery's kitchen — and I realised that I was looking out once again on the ferry.

Heery walked me over a pile of clothes and children's toys and when he got me to the bedroom, he closed the door. "You can stay for a week or so," he said. "If I were you I'd get on to your agent woman."

I said thanks but I wasn't sure if Heery heard.

Heery left and I landed on the bed next to a fat teddy bear. I slept and dreamed of Liska's face, floating in the lull of the sea, tempting me to join her, disappointed with my effort. When I woke, that bear was looking at me from the pillow and I managed to stop myself from tearing it up.

Later, there was a vociferous cheer from the lounge and I began another dream of weeds and pebbles, and Liska lying within. The afternoon advanced to evening, but as I was about to make a move for the door, I was anticipated by a visitor from the Procurator Fiscal's office who picked through the clothes to reach me — a strange visitor who entered backwards and then turned around, every aspect of surprise clear on his face.

The man from the Fiscal was Mr Lash, a tidy official with two circles of heavy glass before his eyes. I felt like asking him to go home. None of it was going to make any difference, but still, a version of the truth would be needed.

"How did you know I was here?" I asked sleepily.

Lash looked at me with more than the expected official disdain. It was a silly question I'd asked, because they know where everybody is these days.

"Was it going to be a dual effort?" he asked.

Lash's stare was about as hard as that of the teddy bear and so I pretended not to know what he was talking about.

"Were you both going to do it?" he said. "Had you both planned to jump?"

Inarticulate, I wasn't even able to say the word no.

"Well," said Lash, "I don't know if it makes a difference. Does it?"

I remembered my story, the same lie I'd been peddling since the islands. In the face of Liska's disappearance and the fact that I'd been sleeping for two days, I had even started to believe it.

"I didn't know she was going to jump," I said.

I looked at the spectacled Mr Lash while he wiped his head and shrugged. "It's not the first time we've seen this," he said, "only normally, one of the parties fails because they're saved. I've not heard of one losing courage."

"It wasn't like that," I said and I pulled the covers up to my neck, a telling gesture. I hid in the bed-sheets and wondered what the script could be:

I tried to stop her really I did.
She'd already gone and I looked about for a life belt.
~~I wasn't ready.~~
She took me by surprise.
~~We never agreed we would actually go through with it.~~

There was nothing I could do.
I wanted to and I tried.

    cf. Andy Warhol : *Suicide (They Won't Let Them Die.*
    Saved in Mid-Air, New York) (1963)   Acrylic and
    silkscreen inks on paper.

"You know best," said Lash. "I'm sorry that she's gone. Sounds
like she was a lovely girl."

"She was," I said.

I was choked but at least it sounded like despair and not guilt.

"You know, my son's out there," said Lash.

The door to the bedroom was part open. Lash looked from one
darkness to the next, into the hall with a moment of expectation.
I had no idea how many rooms this house had because I'd never
counted them. There were constantly new spaces developing in
Heery's home, and people arriving to live in them.

"Our son doesn't live with his family anymore," said Lash, "he
stays down here with you. He's old enough and they say he's very
talented. I just hope he gets somewhere. This looks like a pretty
exhausting place to live."

"Yes," I said, unable to render any hope. The teddy bear stared
with such base knowledge of the situation that I wondered if there
wasn't something wrong with me.

"Is that all part of having talent?" asked the fat man from the
Fiscal. "Why do artists have to live like this?"

"I don't know," I answered.

Lash sighed. He didn't like the lethargy of the house that had
sucked in his son. Heery's old house was the anti-mirror of family
life. But talent always goes south, I thought. Talent shies away from
authority, especially after it's been asked a certain amount of stupid
questions.

"Maybe he'll grow out of it," said Lash. "He keeps telling me that he'll make money. If he does I guess he'll move away from here."

I rested my head, tired by the caution of Mr Lash. Maybe Lash would keep off the obvious questions about Liska and myself so long as I offered some hope of explaining his son's passion for the arts. Lash's kid was an artist however, and it wasn't the poor boy's fault.

"You'd better think about it," said Mr Lash. "Nobody's going to charge you with anything if you tried to save Liska."

He stared into my eyes as I reflected on this. "We all have unsound moments," he said. "You just don't want anyone to suspect you of lying — because if you lie — well then."

I could hear the others talking next door, their voices rising above the clattering mugs.

"If they think you're lying," said Lash, "they won't leave you alone."

I nodded that I had understood, although Mr Lash's attention was now elsewhere.

"He won't talk to me, you know," said Mr Lash.

"Who?" I asked.

"My son won't talk to me anymore."

I didn't move. Lash was trying to make me say something but I didn't know what. I knew that there would be more interviews — friends and family, and officials like I'd never seen — many anxious hours spent in the application of procedure.

"OK," said Mr Lash, and he closed his folder. "I've made a note of what you did and didn't say," he added, and he moved the teddy bear to where it could better watch me.

When the door closed I got out of bed. I was putting my shoes on when Heery entered.

"Yeah," he said, "that was heavy."

"It had a certain mass," I agreed and I went to work on the shoelaces.

Heery asked me if I was going somewhere.

"I need to get out," I said. "Just give me a couple of hours."

I knew that Heery wasn't sure but I carried on with the shoes, and when I was done I walked to where the others were sitting in a heap with their drinks. Everyone fell to a dead hush when I entered.

I recognised the son of Mr Lash immediately, a pretty boy lost in the shabby circumstance of our local artists. "Your dad?" I said and the boy nodded.

He was a funny kid, handsome and teenage, and he had thin arms that looked like they were all rubber and no muscle.

"Nice man," I said and the young Lash shrugged, and returned to the low conversation of the hearth.

25

☐   Later that same day while Heery boiled the hairy tatties that the anarchists called their lunchtime meal, I wandered to the front door of their house and walked down the street, a few experimental metres towards the city. The Victoria Bridge which led from Torry to Aberdeen flashed with cars and lorries, scraps of painted metal which passed at the same speed and in the same direction. I looked to see if I was being followed. I could see the ruined block that Heery, and those others, called a home. It was charming, like a half-broken piano. The upper windows were cracked and the roof was laden with weeds. It was the sort of place officialdom despised because it had no address. It was a house in only a few respects, but I imagined that it had once been very grand. Somewhere in there, Heery (banging on the potlids, blowing in the kettle) sang his praise of green fruits, and I tramped quietly out of the town.

There are different kinds of suicide in this world and only a handful of them result in immediate death. Some suicides drink themselves to death over a forty-year period. Their theatrical side materialises in the emptiness at the end of each drinking bout and in the stagecraft of their decline. Other people, like Liska, are able to get it over with in less than forty seconds.

The sky was chalky and for a moment I was wonderfully unfamiliar with who I was and why I was heading towards the suburbs of Aberdeen, where the city housed its mighty car parks, and the endless ranges of its shopping centres. I arrived at the dual carriageway of the Aberdeen City bypass, or what is more commonly referred to as the Aberdeen Western Peripheral Route — and Liska blinked, sensitive to the spray of the sea — she choked in both her stomach and in her throat, hands upward. Soon it would be her funeral and I didn't want to be around for that.

Trucks hammered along and I followed them for several hours, enough to put distance between myself and those that might want to speak to me. I blasted down the mud of the verge and felt in control once again, my thoughts drowned by the noise of the traffic. The bypass was a satisfying place to grieve, as if the relentless vehicles could give me a real break from people. Only on the bypass did I find within myself the meditative peace that I needed.

> cf. Robert Morris : *Continuous Project Altered Daily* (1969)   Castelli Warehouse, aluminium, asphalt, clay, copper, felt, glass, lead, nickel, rubber, stainless steel, thread, zinc. A world of non-containment.

I stopped when I reached the service station at Clinterty, just as night dawned on the country. The services were a head of brightly-lit concrete, nestled at the foot of Kirkhill Forest. A car park and forecourt were scratched into the evening, and a short row of trucks grimaced as the light failed behind them into the hill. The name of an oil conglomerate pierced the scene from on high, in lines of green brocade, and underneath, lay a tender pattern of grass and bushes.

I walked across the car park, ignorant of the customs of the night and was nearly run down by an expensive motor. Car tyres crept along the ground and shivers ran through every organ. I made it behind the service building and approached the steep area of grass where there was no light — and that's where I lay down — up a grass slope and behind the cafeteria.

I crawled to sleep. This was my bush for the night, a warm six-legged stamen of a root with a flowered head of green. It was comfortable but the moment that I dozed, under the pins and needles of the night, I heard the mourning voice of Liska.

My eyes wouldn't close, you see, it was as if the lids would only rest, and although it was night time, there was still too much light intruding. My feet buzzed, fortified with bad blood, all the protein of the day settling in my soles like fatty acid. My teeth stuck together like their wood had melted with sugar. It was the first time Liska properly visited me after her death, and she was ready with the question I most feared.

"Why didn't you jump when you had the chance?" she said.

"I don't know," I answered. "I wasn't ready. I couldn't figure it out. I was in love with you. I wanted to be an artist."

"Not until you're dead," she said. "You can't be an artist until you're dead. In the meantime, artistic lifestyle is a contradiction."

"Don't say that," I said to Liska. "I feel so guilty."

I watched Liska float across my vision and wondered if she was right.

An engine blew to life in the car park and I opened my eyes in time to see a silo-sized bubble of lead exhaust blow up from a nearby lorry. I didn't dare think about being forgiven for what I had failed to do, and so I dozed in that old bush at the back of the service station, settled on the damp ground within earshot of the road. The sound of the road became that of an organ pipe, it rose and died and renewed like the drone of an emergency warning — and I was at rest — almost at home, having found limbo once again.

26

■ What light came across the landscape in the morning did so as a formality. The sound of vehicles blew heavy in the distance. There had never been anything on this site except a rocky field, until at some point in our recent history, some people in protective suits had arrived and laid a concrete basin, a car park and a service station, and then gone off down the road to do the same, 50 miles further south.

I clapped my body for a little strength, but that didn't work. I was stiff and my clothes had stuck. When I'd set out the day before I had thought that it would take me several days to arrive at this state, but, after only one night, I was impossibly abandoned to the world of wretchedness which lurks — I tell you now — only centimetres below our modern senses.

> cf. Damien Hirst : *A Thousand Years* (1991) Steel, glass,
> flies, maggots, MDR, insect-o-cutor, cow's head, sugar,
> water.

When men built service stations and roads, they replaced nature with a bacteriological muck. What had been green then became brown. Rivers were filled with lumpy mud, forests replaced with poles, shafts and spikes — roadways were driven in compass lines through the eeriness — and the speed limit was set at 70. Nature wasn't needed anymore, not once the car was in production. Nature was now to be experienced through a medium.

In the service station at Clinterty, lorries revved up clouds of oily smoke and the smell of metaplastic bread rose from the back of the cafeteria. I crawled to rest within the stem of my bush. I didn't want anyone to see me.

When the sun made its official appearance, I stretched my legs and thought about Liska's funeral and the fact that people would soon be trying to get her paintings. I doubted that her funeral could go ahead until a proper cause of death had been stated and, given that I was the chief witness, I could see matters being held up indefinitely. If they came after me for questioning, I daresay I'd give in. Even if they dreamed up a charge like Perversion of Suicide, I daresay I'd pass beneath the battlements of the law — and give in.

The morning passed but I was not brave enough to move. That's how long it takes for you to become untenable in this world — just one night away from goose feather and soap and you're a savage who needs to be hosed down. Civilisation is only some fine letters and curls standing in the middle of a swamp.

On top of that, Liska's washed-away body now stood out clearly against the dark surface of Kirkhill Forest, and she was frowning at me, signalling for me to join her. All the aches of the night were back in place and worse than before. I shut my eyes and tried to sleep but my skin was too cold.

Why wasn't Liska annoyed with me?

It's typical of dreams to be so unfaithful.

Liska was mid-tumble, falling towards the water and her life was racing before her eyes and she didn't even know that I wasn't there beside her. She didn't even know that I was alive and that I'd gone all the way to Lerwick and back to Aberdeen.

I cuddled against my knees. It was dark again and car lights inscribed dashes along the road. The trousers of yesterday had become consumptive damp strips that would never mend and I had stopped collecting information about the world outside. As I stood up, the mechanics of my stiff body picked together into the slim assessment of my health. All the pain-intensive systems of my hunger kicked in and I was ready to go for the very first time into the noisy world of the road service.

27

☐ The traffic fluttered past and a clot of cold spread up my legs. A truck under the canopy came jogging to a halt — a man jumped out and stretched — and that was the excitement over. The darkened bypass was enlarged by occasional headlights, and I walked to the window of the service building and was seen in the glass to be disgusting. Life was rejecting me at last.

cf.   T.T. Macoutes : *Hand That Emits Tears* (2001)
Painted acorn wood on aluminium base.

In the cafeteria, the toilets were empty so I kicked away my shoes and dropped my shirt. I collected paper towels and started on my body with hot water, balancing with one foot on the tiles. Liska could have moved at any moment, lifted a hand from the seabed and clicked her fingers slowly — and that crackling would have been enough to cause a calamity. With a rumble, another service station would sink into the earth — the victim of a dead artist's deepest repulsions.

All of which destruction would be justified, I thought as I took off my underwear. We demarcate everything and everybody gets a label. No one can escape, I thought as my underpants dropped to the wet floor of the toilet. We are all as bad as each other. Our concerns might clash, but we're not doing anything about the real problem — which is our own lack of contentment.

Using paper towels, I wiped my bottom and thought about Anna Lunken. In most ways, I realised, Anna Lunken was a more perfect citizen than I could ever be. Anna Lunken is not one thing and then the other — she is all of one thing, I thought as I wiped my bush-sore bum. Anna Lunken knows that ignorance is peril and that if you don't put your own needs first, you'll either end up dead in the sea, or dancing naked in a roadside toilet.

I cleaned up my privates and threw the paper towels in the bin. I jumped up and belted my leg out — and it felt good. I should do this more often, I thought. I took a couple of turns around the tiled floor, almost at a loss without clothes, unsure of which way to turn, and completely excited.

An instinct had awakened and I had arrived at a crossroads.

Everything was a possibility and once again I felt refreshed.

I jumped up and spun around again.

Liska skimmed across the surface of the sea, and she raised her hand and laughed.

When the door to the toilets opened, I picked up my trousers as if nothing was going on. The dirty-looking guy who came in wore a lorry-driver's badge and I made a short pretence of cleaning myself. The guy glanced but that was it — he'd seen worse than me naked in a toilet so I figured that everything was all right.

When the lorry guy had finished pissing and washing his hands, I had all my clothes on and I cleared my throat and tried my luck.

"Do you know how I can get a ride back to Aberdeen?" I asked.

The guy looked at me, good and long, depressive as a rain-soaked cow. His moustaches drooping into a beard that looked like it wouldn't grow in the proper places.

"You're a freak," he said after a moment. He spoke like an islander.

"I was just washing," I said to him, "I've been sleeping in a bush."

"You're still a freak," he said.

"I know that," I said, "but I just need a lift back to Aberdeen."

The lorry-driver looked at me and I could feel a decision in the offing. His hands roamed back and fore across his belly as he dried them on his shirt.

"I'll fix you up," he said, "but I'll need to search you first."

"Search me?" I asked. "You've seen I've nothing to hide."

The driver didn't laugh — he only said, "Nobody likes freaks." The comment came with a meaningful stare.

He turned to leave and I followed him. I never knew his real name because when I asked him he said nothing and pointed to a seat in the cafeteria, meaning that I should sit down. Nobody likes freaks and I didn't like him either. He ordered everything on the menu as if it were an eating contest and I watched it all go down.

"Come on," he said when he'd finished.

I was dreaming of my darkened bush retreat. There had been some happy hours up there. At least that was the way it seemed as I climbed into the cab and felt the engine vibrate in unexpected places.

The driver made no effort to speak so I sat back and felt sad about everything as the vehicle took to the road, terrified that from my passenger seat I could see over the warped, blackish tops of the other road vehicles. This is how I returned to Aberdeen. The sound of the engine was so deep that everything took on a proper place and harmony. I dropped to sleep but a bump on the road kicked up my head. I looked around and the driver was staring down the carriageway like it was a shooting range.

When the end of the ride came, the driver made a gruff noise, which meant that I was to get out. I was on the north side of Aberdeen among the old sheds and weeds again, with the smell of oil, standing in a long commercial lot where rows of lorries rested like mortified caterpillars.

I closed the lorry's door, which was nearly impossible and the driver looked out of his window and said "Good luck, squire," and that was about the most he'd offered in his life.

28

■ The low moon between the tower blocks at the Bridge of Don showed that it was dawn. A chill rose from the drains. Every curtain was closed in the concrete fortification which faced the dual carriageway where the lorry had stopped. The graffiti and boarded windows indicated that this part of the world had been left behind by the farting winds of progress long ago. In the first light the stiff and flat architecture suggested vagueness and mystery. Only the moon floated, radiant and fading in the light, dripping its silver paint on the ugliest of buildings.

A vein in my forehead was telling me that soon I'd need a drink or some breakfast and after, I'd need to be shacked up and in some semblance of a bed.

As I walked towards Aberdeen city centre, occasionally canting to the left and right to share the weight of my body between my feet, I reached a street of dingy brick houses plastered with advertisements.

When a train rumbled by and shook the brittle iron struts of a nearby bridge, its noise was joined by a tattered electric smell which seemed both terribly familiar and exotic. The noises were more insistent as I reached a main road. The vehicles here seemed to offer some warm humidity in the cold, their engines muffled and highly soporific. All that could be distinguished from the windows of the cars were steering wheels on hands and black, open mouths. Far in the distance I could make out the summits of those bright buildings that made up the city, and so I increased my step and settled into a steady march.

cf. Wolf Vostell : *Theatre is in the Street* (1958) Paris, auto parts and a television.

Walking by myself — talking to myself — thinking my thoughts out loud — like the romantic view I'd taken of the situation — it could only last so long. Progressive illumination delineated first the outline of full human expressions in the cars and as the daylight appeared, each particular facet of the town also became subject to the same gradual clarification. Closed shops and railings — car parks and cafes and with them the first individuals of the day, appearing on the broken pavements and each consigned to their own mission. They had only just risen.

> cf. Yuan Chai and Jian Jun Xi : *Two Naked Men Jump Into Tracey's Bed* (1999) The men had a pillow fight on Tracey Emin's *My Bed* for around fifteen minutes, to applause from the crowd, before being removed by security guards.

The further I walked towards the city centre, past marshalling yards and cold stores — the more people joined me. The people were unfamiliar at first, dark, as if they wore gowns, masks and hoods — but at seven o'clock the sun appeared and I became a part of the crowd — all of us heading in the same direction. When the freeze thawed after eight o'clock, the vehicles came in one large blast. The sound formed a cone that positively hummed — and I realised that everyone was converging on the same thing. More cars appeared from a tiny dream-hole in the distance and they charged along beside us, forming a stream towards the harbour. The night was a masterpiece and the dawn was a defacement giving a jaundiced tinge to the city.

> cf. Vladimir Umanets : *Deface of Mark Rothko's Black on Maroon* (2012) Black ink on oil on canvas. Drab Yellowist public relations.

I saw Liska again too, when the ringing song of the traffic became a drone in my ear. When one car joined another, and each face sat hunched with chin on steering wheel, I saw Liska again. The tide bore Liska's hair and the seaweed formed her dress. Liska's forehead was white and her skin was cracked with cold, and her eyes darted to the left to see me. In the gravity of the water there was nothing for Liska to do but float. The sea was endless and the current pulled her around, turning her with the stream. Tiny fish picked at her arms and her skin floated away like chunks of cork.

"All of this awaits us," said Liska. "Join me if you can, Guy."

Liska hit the waters of the North Sea. If there was one vision that would not stop repeating in the surge of thought as I stood on the wide-open of the Castlegate, it was Liska flying from the back of the ferry.

It was with this in mind that I picked myself up and headed west towards Aberdeen's office accommodation. I was thinking that I had better have a drink, even though it was barely nine o'clock.

"Turn around, son! What a fucking mess you look — what sort of a pair of trousers are those? Is that the way y'all dress now?"

With such words was I greeted by a traffic warden — a parking attendant by another name. Actually, I noticed that his jacket had Parking Supervisor printed on it, which maybe meant that he had three jobs. The traffic warden had a gopher's face and waited at a jammed road junction. I looked down the creases of my trousers, along a brown streak which I recognised as roadside mud from my service station. All that my pissy roadside bush had impressed upon my clothes had hardened into discoloured beads of mud. This was grief as I had never known it, and yet I was still telling myself that everything was all right. With my narrow eyes arching in different directions, I tried to see my reflection in a shop window. I was the real portrait of despair.

cf. Gavin Turk : *Oi* (1998) 3 R-type photographs, overall 96 x 240 inches

I shrugged.

"Stay! Let me have a good look at you," said the attendant.

I presented myself to this parking attendant, sure that I wasn't all that bad — although he had his own ideas.

"Gordon Bennett, son," he said, "where the hell you from?"

I looked with some confusion at my coat and trousers. All answers seemed non-potential until I remembered that I was from Aberdeen.

The traffic warden led me from the pavement, courteous but very firm. "A flipping joke," I heard him say as he squeezed my arm, "what's going on with you?"

To my enclosed and neurotic mind, unsuited to talking to public officials, I had no recourse but to answer with the shocking truth. "I'm running away," I said — although it sounded embarrassing.

The traffic warden led me by the arm.

"I'm looking for somewhere to rest," I said, another psychotically irrelevant contribution. "I'm an artist," I added, as if this would help make my case. It did.

"I know you're an artist," said the gopher-like traffic warden. "I used to be an artist too," he added grimly, "— but it's no life. It just doesn't get you anywhere, innit?"

My brains turned dry and hot. I realised what it was I'd first noticed about this parking attendant, the singular air of reluctance he had and the fact that, even in his uniform, he looked mad. The man had a hopeful air, like a rodent sniffing the atmosphere for what was coming.

"Why are you doing this if you're an artist?" I asked.

"It's quite easy," he said. "Sickened by my incapacity to sell even one single work of art, I ended up quitting the artistic life and getting a job. It ain't that uncommon round here."

I watched my new friend as he lit a half cigarette. He pointed at the Castlegate Café across the road, its windows obscure and invisible with a coating of dirt and dust.

"Come and join me," he said. "Have a cup of tea and find out all about it."

29

☐ I paused on the doormat of the Castlegate Café, jarred and shaken by the transition from cold to warmth and surprised by the amazing amount of traffic wardens within. Away from the rattling metal of the café's tea urns, I counted no less than four tables of traffic wardens, all of whom were immersed in deep debate.

"This way," said my guide, and we walked through the clatter of plates and the tinkle of conversation. The table we reached had two spaces remaining and a pile of peaked caps in the centre. We joined an animated argument that was at first hard for me to follow.

"Forget your ambition," the warden next to me was saying. "Failure is the new success."

"It's bullshit," came a booming voice from the other side of the table. "Your irony's a little too obvious — even for this crowd."

The faces and ages and sizes of the six parking supervisors at this table varied, but their passion was consistent. My comrade ordered two teas and two rolls, while I gazed hopelessly around. A quieter table of older traffic wardens drowsed and smoked, greasy after their breakfasts. Above them a pool of smoke hung round a limp fan, while rusting mirrors reflected cracked corners of plaster and damp.

"I went to college too," said a traffic warden wiping a scarlet curtain of ketchup from his lip. "I figured I could take two years of eating Mac and cheese, but I ended up doing four. I worked in hospitals and retail. In two years I got one meaningful piece done, some nudes, like. I saved money and made offset prints of the scenes and that took about two months each after work. Imagine tight crosshatching with the .005 micron pigma pen on picture fields 18 x 24 inch? I made 500 copies of each of my first four out of six. Signed and numbered them all, plaque-mounted a mix of 100 prints, packaged, shrink wrapped, Styrofoam corners and all that.

They worked out at about 60 quid each for about a 20 quid per unit production cost. I've still got most of them in the house. Now you tell me I didn't work hard enough."

All the traffic wardens wanted to speak at the same time but it was my friend the gopher who was the loudest.

"You could have lived with yer parents!" he said. "No need to get a job then, Mikey!"

Mikey shook his head doubtfully but what he said was drowned in a melee of protest at the idea of parental contribution. It was one of the older ones who was heard.

"I did some abstract paintings for my senior show," he said, "but that was thirty years ago, mate. I can't paint like that anymore anyway. I can't even paint on canvas anymore. It's too rectangulary — know what I mean? So I paint on ribbed cardboard, which no one'll ever hang in a gallery. Who'd buy a painting on ribbed cardboard? I'm just saying you've got to stick to yer guns — that's all."

"And I'm saying you should give up," said Mikey, frowning.

"This is Guy," said my friend. "I think he needs a job."

"We all need a job!" said the traffic warden to my right, a man drinking tea with his coat collars turned up.

I held my hand up in welcome and received a few nods from the crowd. One of the traffic wardens who hadn't spoken laid his folded napkin down and addressed the table in a quiet and innocent fashion.

"For me," he said, "art's more a release of emotion than a profession. So I can still work as an artist and do this. Art works itself out to precise lines of creativity and as long as I'm doing that I'm succeeding — that's what I think — anyway."

"Fuck you," said a fat traffic warden, scratching his ear with a cigarette. "Art's not art until it's sold — you know that — I know that — even Thinger Boy over there knows that — don't kid yourself otherwise."

I had to agree but I wouldn't have put it quite so harshly,

especially given the obvious sensitivity of the parking attendant who'd been speaking. He seemed up to the challenge however, and addressed Fatty with his folded napkin.

"I've had art shows," he said in his quiet voice, "— and I've received the highest praise an artist can get — my work as a tattoo on someone else's skin. It's not that I don't lack the potential to sell — I just lack the public. Not everyone can make it."

Fatty turned to his breakfast and shrugged.

"We'd all be best givin' up, is all," he said — and he bit his roll, releasing a trickle of egg which ran into the beans on his plate — creating an effect much like an artist's palette, I thought.

One more traffic warden, the proud owner of a snazzy goatee, had something to say. "Ahmad doesn't think it's dishonourable, not selling your art," he said, tilting his head back so that he appeared humorously pretentious. "He just likes doing art because it saves him going to counselling — isn't that right? I mean he's getting it out of his system, in'ee?"

The quiet-spoken attendant motioned awkwardly with his head, neither a nod nor a shake. "I'm not sure about the counselling," he said. "Art's certainly a path of emotional passage and one that we all need to make, whether for commercial reasons or no."

Fatty snorted and finished his roll.

"Don't make you an artist, is all," he said, egg visible on his lip. "You's just using art for you's own ends, not even bothering to think about an audience or a market. All I'm just saying is that when I'm doing art I'm under no illusions, and I'm in it to make ends meet. I do what I love — and now I can't — so instead I write up tickets — and maybe that'll stop — and maybe someone'll buy one of my paintings and I might be able to give up this crappy lot."

"I'm an artist too," said snazzy goatee, "— and I say we should all stick to us guns and take the rough with the smooth. Not that there's ever an ounce of smooth. But we're artists — and we have to survive as artists — because you never know — somebody might take an interest."

From the looks around the table I understood that all present had heard this kind of platitude before, and a few of them sucked their breath in and nodded.

"I once gave a parking ticket to Tracy Emin," said one, "— but she framed it and it sold for £6,000."

"That's fame," said Fatty — and, as if this word had jogged his memory, he turned his plumpness to me and said: "Have you ever sold anything?"

"I had a couple of bits in a show this year," I told him. "I had this idea that my art wasn't going to be for sale though. My girlfriend thought the same."

I thought he was going to have diao-here-eeah, the way he jumped.

"I'm sorry," said my gopher-faced companion, "but that's pretty much a new one! You'll have to tell us about it sometime."

"I will," I said — and they frowned, and a few of them muttered about money and value, and once more, how art was not art until it had been sold. The conversation broke up and the traffic wardens gathered their hats and began to squeeze out of the door.

Outside, it was time to work. During our breakfast, motor cars had parked in every last corner and the shop-lights had ignited. The traffic wardens gathered in groups and adjusted their belts, making phone calls and bursting into high, light laughs. Roughly moulded lumps of cloud dotted the horizon and on the street, pedestrians stared with cold, level glances at the traffic lights, waiting for their turn to move. My new friend the gopher stood next to me, stretched himself and positioned his parking attendant's hat upon his head. I smiled at him, but he merely caressed his wrist several times.

"I've hurt my hand," he said, "— the ticket machines hurt your hands — but it's not as if they don't tell you — but this injury in my hand — there isn't an official channel through which you can — do you know what I mean? You can't just stand up for yourself —"

The gopher didn't finish speaking. He looked at his hand as if he'd just unwrapped it from a parcel. I watched with a minimum of attention, lolling apathetically against the café wall, watching the wardens depart in different directions.

The gopher told me his name — "Parry."

I shook the wounded hand of Parry and participated in close-quarters examination.

"I'm Guy," I said, and I drank from my plastic cup of tea, accidentally slobbering some of it onto my shirt.

"Where are you headed?" asked Parry, now raising the elevated arcs of his eyebrows into a pair of question marks. "'Cause I'm going up the west end."

I looked along a line of traffic into the glittering folds of light in the distance, where the cars' lights and the natural light combined into a low level twinkle.

"I don't know," I answered.

"I'll be in the Prince of Wales at one o'clock," he said, "if you want to carry on the conversation."

"One o'clock," I said, and I nodded in agreement, energised by my breakfast.

I departed for my wander, drifting between the people on Union Street and uplifted by the alien austerity of so many empty shops, and from a good few metres away, I turned and waved goodbye to Parry, who with considerable deliberation, was already deciding whether or not to book a certain van.

30

■   The Prince of Wales pub had a wide frontage with two doorways flanked by great bay windows.

"I need to decide if I should go back to work," said Parry as I met him at the appointed hour — and he pushed the door pensively, a distant look in his eyes. He walked in with his numerous hand-held meters and devices hanging limply from his belt.

"Did you give out any tickets this morning?" I asked by way of conversation, and Parry nodded and then bid me silent.

The venue for our debauch was fuller than I expected. Most of the people in the Prince were lunching office workers, which I found moderately shocking, as they were all getting drunk. Within minutes I was drinking wine, tired out by my wanderings around the junctions, terraces and concrete corners of Aberdeen.

"What have you been doing all morning?" asked Parry, and I told him that I had been waiting for this drink.

We knocked glasses and Parry gave me a look that made me sure we were going to be friends. He seemed strange, but kind nonetheless.

"Were you really an artist once?" Parry asked once he'd downed most of a glass of stout and typed some rude words into his hand-held ticket machine.

"Maybe I still am," I said.

"What are you going to do for trousers?" he asked, indicating my mud-streaked strides, morbidly pasted to my legs where they were still wet.

I didn't have any compunction about sharing my master plan. "I'm going to steal some," I said.

"Gosh," was Parry's answer — and with it he removed his lip from his drink and ordered two more— along with shots of vodka.

I drank the vodka and thought of Liska, and the thought receded as the alcohol burned. I looked at my shoes and felt sad, because my shoes reminded me of Liska too. I had considered these same shoes when I'd been standing in the dark, waiting over the North Sea, while Liska floated away below. Was that her voice I heard? Could she scream something up to me before she drowned?

"That's brave," said Parry — and I looked into his face — into his mind.

"I have to get some new shoes too," I confided, and Parry nodded, looking back to his hand with a macabre interest.

"Have you ever sold anything?" he asked.

Around us, lunchers poured brown and red sops onto bowls of fried foods and salad. Light glowed in the high windows, and toasted cheeses were passed across into several quick hands. The Prince was panelled and mirrored and hung with ornamental tin advertising plates up to its curious ceiling. The ceiling was ribbed like the inside of a ship's hull, and revealed many unsecured wiring connections.

"I haven't sold a thing," I said. "But you don't need to sell to be an artist — really. It's not easy being an artist these days — so I never sold anything — and that was a point of principle."

I began to feel anxious. An octopoidal monster was feeling for my neck — reaching from below my shirt and squeezing me of air — as if with each word I was found more guilty. I tried to straighten Liska's idea in my mind once more but for the time being she'd gone, leaving me to improvise on her original theme.

"It's not art until it's sold," said Parry — and it felt like the umpty-umpth time I'd heard that answer.

"Where did you hear that?" I asked, but he shrugged.

"I didn't hear it anywhere. It's just a truth — isn't it?"

"What about all the art that children make?" I asked. "What about public art and art happenings?"

Parry unhooked his ticket machine from his belt and rested it on the bar. "For children everything is a rehearsal," he said, "and as for the rest, folks get paid to make public art and do their silly happenings. They're all in it for the money. They have to be."

Determined to prove a point I asked Parry to follow me and led him to the end of the bar, where I picked up a knife, fork and a wineglass.

"Piss into this," I said, "and meet me outside in five minutes."

Pocketing the knife and fork I exited the bar and strolled up to Union Street, hiccupping fast. In the nearest shop I found what I was looking for in their reasonably well-stocked baking section — a plastic tub of sugar sprinkles — and I purchased these and joined Parry once again, outside. Parry held the glass of urine by the stem.

"Won't be a minute," I said, leading Parry down the pavement beside the Prince of Wales in search of the nearest curl of dog poo. This being downtown Aberdeen, we didn't have to walk far until we found one — a fresh cheek of dog waste that lay low on the kerb. I bid Parry look.

"All I do is place the fork and knife on either side," I said, "position the wine glass to the upper right and then sprinkle."

And breaking the seal on my sprinkles (the label called them 'coloured sugar cake decorations') I showered the dog waste with a rainbow of colours, completing the piece.

Parry was amused but he wasn't to be led. He tried to take a picture of my artwork with his mobile phone, which appeared to be out of power — and walking back to the Prince, he shrugged and offered me his verdict.

"You've proved my point, but not yours," he said. "That wasn't art — it was just a joke. The difference is negligible these days, I know — but you'll never make a career out of it — not unless you can get someone to offer you a grant — or find someone to buy what you just did — which I doubt will happen."

I doubted it too, that had to be said — and yet I wondered if someone would buy my sprinkled dog dirt if my name was Warhol.

I held up my hands and followed Parry back to the pub. Our drinks were waiting when we walked in and I refused to speak for several minutes, brooding over the injustice of it all. When late lunch reached its zenith, a crowd of young men came in and started on the sandwiches and brown ales. There were about ten of them and the burly crowns of their heads circled the bar. Parry moved his parking attendant's hat under the table and indicated the lunchers to me.

"My clients," he said, glaring angrily from his corner.

The young businessmen were a cool and brutal breed. Their faces were angry — their hands were forks — their bellies were drums of pasta — their hair was waterproof — their voices were off the Beaufort scale — their walk was that of churchmen — and their shoes were the peel of the finest fruits.

"Let's go to another bar," said Parry, who was eyeing up the young businessmen as well. "I'm scared to stay here any longer. And I'm definitely not going back to work today."

We left the Prince of Wales for another pub, where we drank some more beer and talked some more about what was art and what was not. God knows we would never find out, but that was what we wanted to talk about. Later in the afternoon Parry turned to wine, and when he did, I made to go, but he insisted that I stay.

"I like talking about art," he said, and as it was 6pm he switched off his radio, the one that had been interrupting us with inanities such as 'Four-five to base,' all afternoon. He dug into his tobacco and rolled a trumpet-shaped cheroot, which he stuck in his mouth.

"Have you got a home to go to?" he asked and he clapped me on the head.

"No," I said and slumped on to the bar.

"Don't worry," he said. "I want to talk some more so we can go back to mine."

"Oh yeah?" I asked.

Parry nodded and got more drinks in. The subject of art and artists fascinated him.

"When people moan about the poor state of the arts today," he said, "they generally blame the artists." He had settled in and I gave him my full attention. "The artists should paint better or go for less of the conceptual stuff — people say. Artists have no ideas and they just won't paint properly — they say. And see those artists? They're always talking pretentious, arty rubbish, pleased that whatever they do, they can justify it with a few clever words. It's not the problem though," said Parry, and he swirled his glass.

"What is the problem?" I asked.

"Drink," he said, and he drank it down.

Parry beat his fingers on the bar and chewed on his cigarette, still not lighting it.

"Some folks are born to a good living," he said. "I am a trained artist, and I made some errors long ago, and now I'm stuck with it. But I could have worked in the oil industry — or I could have invented a new gadget. Or I could have started a business. The thing is, though, that when you become an artist you opt out of certain social skills."

I gazed into my glass of wine and imagined the disarming grunt of the French farmer who had grown it. There was the soil on his boot — the sparking of his tractor engine. There was the press and there was the lorry taking the wine out of the country. There, in the wineglass, I noticed, was Liska floating through some seaweed, her hands full of sand.

"You're right," I said, unsure what I was agreeing with. "Can I really stay at yours tonight? I will tell you my sorry tale if you want."

"Okay," he said, "you can stay — I've got a couch in the studio —" and the words filled my mind because they were the best things I had ever heard.

I heard those words all right but as they echoed in my mind,

Liska came too — crossing the dunes and creeks of the seabed, pulling herself along the curve of a sandbank to see what I was doing. I waited but Liska wouldn't leave me. She hung about in the debris of the seabed and asked if I was dead yet — and I made my excuses and carried on drinking — and talking about art — pleased that I would be passing out on a long soft couch sometime soon.

31

☐   When I got to Parry's Rosemount flat, the couch was covered in newspaper. He grabbed the nearest page and waved it as he searched under his living room table for more drink.

"Liska," he said. "She's dead — and you're famous. I hadn't heard of either of you before she died. But now I know all about you. Look at that!"

"How do you reckon I'm famous?" I asked.

"I know who you are," said Parry, "— but don't worry — I'm a big fan of what you and Liska did."

As Parry poured me a tumbler of sea-dark wine, I read the article in the newspaper, amazed at the pictures on display. Parry passed me some more cuttings, and said "See!"

It was awesome — Liska had hit the big time. There were many sheets of newspaper on Parry's couch and Liska was in them all. There was even an example of my work in one of the papers which had opted to present the Liska story in a two page photospread. Parry threw aside his parking supervisor's peaked hat and dashed off to change his clothes, and I drank my wine and flicked through the cuttings.

There were no surprises. All the small silver beings of the art world had begun their games the very second that Liska's death had become known, with Mr Sharma leading the charge. From the papers I gathered that after Liska had died, Mr. Sharma had steered his showboat from the centre of the channel towards the bank, while the art-lovers waited in speechless wonder for the miracle of her work — which Mr Sharma had announced that he would sell. Everyone had something to say about the death of Liska and, as is sometimes the case in the newspapers, there was something weirdly pre-ordained about the blow by blow post-mortem consummation.

There was another renaissance coming — all the papers agreed with that. Art was always exhibited with a characteristic know-it-all standing beside it telling us about its nuances, tones and swings, and Liska's death was no exception. Mr Sharma was one of these know-it-alls and he appeared in several of the newspapers explaining Liska's work. Liska had achieved artistic status at last and even more, one of the papers pronounced stoically in a short column:

> *The tragic death of artist Liska this week was followed by calls to improve the safety records of our North Sea ferries, which over the last year have hosted similar fatalities.*

A flake of foam fluttered to the surface of the water and the art world continued pretty much as per usual, making a whole lot of fuss about very nearly nothing.

> cf. Paul Struth : *No Work Today* (2001) House keys, one pint of milk [to be changed each four days], daily newspaper [to be changed each day].

It took an hour for Liska to drop. I hung like a gargoyle from the back of the ferry and the guilt began at that very lonely moment. Liska was in the sea and she must have been wondering where I was and why I couldn't be there with her — and even while I read Parry's newspapers, I could still hear her call. I closed my eyes and there she was in the water. I shared the same sight, the view of the ferry, travelling away from her. Liska was under the water and alone. The air was punched out of her and she was conscious in a new way. At that point there was only one thing that mattered to Liska and it was that I was there with her, in the sea.

Liska surfaced and felt like she had nearly lost her breath. The next shock she experienced was the wake of the ferry and the way it rolled her up and over. At that point, Liska's only thought was to wonder where I was. The thought departed and Liska went under again and couldn't feel her feet. She wanted to shout my name but she was too cold to shout. Rising and falling above the surface of the sea, Liska recalled some of life's sensations — being penniless — a shot of light from a car window — the sadness of her family. Liska knew that I hadn't jumped with her, and she watched the ferry leave, that huge ship becoming tiny very quickly. I was stuck to the railing of the ship as if by frost and when somebody grabbed me, that was when I closed my eyes.

That's exactly what happened — I closed my eyes. When Liska jumped from the ferry, I couldn't even bear to look — far less act. I could only shed tears. The tears were all I had to prove myself — and I heard a voice.

"Let go."

It was a clear-as-a-bell voice from the back of my mind.

"Jump," said the voice, "you jump now."

My tears fell and I didn't let go, despite the voice. I couldn't prise my hands off that boat, then or ever. Watching the ferry, Liska let out a long breath and realised that she'd coped with the fall. All Liska thought about as she watched the boat travel away, was how long she had to wait. The sea was noisier than she had thought. Even in the middle of the sea, away from the boat, the water gleamed black, flexing muscle and swelling.

It was only when I was held by someone that I pretended to fall, as if I were about to jump. The man who held me had anticipated me. I've not been able to face the memory of that man without turning it away, because in that moment I pretended that I had to follow Liska. I tried to follow Liska but the next thing I knew was that I'd failed to act, and she had gone.

I gasped for breath.

Sometimes Liska dies as soon as she hits the water but I know that's just a fiction. I know that however hard Liska falls she's always going to come to the surface and wonder where I am.

In fact Liska didn't even break a limb — she was treading water — and she even wondered if she could be there for hours. When she was waiting in the water like that, Liska wondered if she should swim a little, but she couldn't get any purchase. If she tried to move, she was always pushed away and there was no way to control her direction.

The sound of the sea. For me it's like heaven, ethereal and yet loud, like a crashing aeroplane. Every day I hear stories of drowning — such anecdotes seek me out. Drowned lovers in the local river, and the sinking of fishing boats and ferries — I can't pass a radio without hearing another story of a drowned person. The passive enjoyment of the sound of the sea isn't possible for me anymore, and if I sit in a chair to concentrate on something else, you bet it'll creep up on me. I can't go to the beach because the sea makes such an alarming gulp. It lifts Liska to the top of a wave and throws her down again. There's a silent place between the waves sometimes, and Liska looks above and sees the stars — cold stars meditating on her. Look at that girl, a drop in the ocean.

I think of the end of Liska's life as one short and revolutionary moment. Liska's head goes under the water where it's quieter and finally she says 'help'. Funny, but 'help' may be one of the few words we learn with conviction — the one word we may never say, or maybe only say the once.

"Help," said Liska — and it didn't matter that no other person could hear, because the word gave her brief warmth. I thought of Liska as I'd remembered her, smiling at me from her studio — but she'd finally gone. True loneliness was Liska's because she'd managed to say the word at last: "Help."

■   In an arena now molten with a shortage of ideas and the crackling wood of spent fires, I see Liska as if walking on the leading edge of a world-ending tsunami, the Pale Woman herself — now radiantly calm — all trace of former worry spent — holding forth her hand for me to grasp that I may be borne up out of the deadly rictus of the art world. I hear Liska's steady voice, the epitome of care, as in a tone of the sweetest collusion she recommends that I place my consciousness in her safe-keeping, at least until I reach —

And here she indicates the shell of a person I have become, reminding me that my days are numbered. All the projects that were dreamed of but never built — all the art that has disappeared — the sudden irruption of our love again into what has hitherto been a hypnosis of slow-motion stolidity — I see Liska's face and I long to make amends — and I admit that I was very scared of doing so then.

"Try it," she seems to say, inexpressibly buoyant in death — but I moved on — hidden for the time being in Aberdeen, anonymous for the time being and in the company of the parking attendants, who surprised me with their taste, their patience and their dedication to grassroots art.

☐ As Parry left for his day on the streets of Aberdeen, I got to my feet. "Can I stay again tonight?" I said. "You mightn't know it but you saved my soul. I haven't anywhere else to go."

"Yeah," said Parry. "That's OK. I gotta pump the pavements for some more hours. Then I'll see you." Parry was weary beyond expression and played with his fake tie.

> cf. Conrad Treger : *Für Schweine und Menschen* (1999 – 2001) Treger dressed over 40 animals in custom-made business suits and had them attend policy meetings for his future projects.

"I'll be here at five o'clock," he said. "I'm gonna lock you out, so do what you can. I gotta book some traffic."

Parry left me on the step and I waited there and closed my eyes, perhaps still asleep, perhaps still drunk. I heard Liska bubbling from that vague porch of gloom from where she watched me, and when I peeped through my hands I saw her jaw spring open behind a screen of black weeds.

"You're not going to get away with this," said Liska — and she snapped off one of her fingers and pointed it at me.

"Not now," I said.

When Liska let go of the finger it floated towards me, magnified by the deep. The finger lingered in the waters — an accusation. Liska looked everlastingly at me.

"This is hopeless," she said.

Liska's bone-white face was close. There were no eyes and no skin. She was dead but I still found her attractive. I swallowed and stared at her. It wasn't the easiest thing to interpret the empty skull of a dead woman.

"Don't you understand that I'm missing you?" said Liska.

I pressed my hands to my head while Liska spoke from the tongue of the ocean, strange dead requests that I could not stop my ears against.

"Go and get some clean trousers for my funeral," she said, and I snapped awake. It was most unlike Liska to talk about my clothes so I felt I had to respond, or at least make a pretense of action.

"I haven't any money left," I said, and at that moment realised I was talking to nobody but myself.

When I arrived in the city centre shortly afterwards, I found a department store and started towards the menswear as if I were a traditional shopper. One plastified face after another passed me as I walked through the tender colours of the furniture department. Slow moving purchasers turned as if hypnotised, unable to differentiate between themselves and the mirrors. Besides the great operations of ritual magic contained in this store, there were numerous processes of a minor and vulgar order that brought me back to life. In a second, with a bruised stare from Liska's eyeless sockets, I had woken to another opportunity. Between underwear and menswear, Liska aimed my attention at the security guard following me.

"The exits of hell are the entrances of paradise," she said.

"That's meaningless," I answered.

"No it's not," she said. "Think of the inevitability of what you're doing."

"I can't join you down there," I told her.

"And you're all very boring up there," she said. "Are you going to steal those trousers or not?"

Liska stared from the water and I retreated from the security guard and snuck free of that shop, and began to think of how better to get warm clothes. Later, I arrived at a charity shop and chose some pennyweight items — the trousers of an older man and a pair of rainbow-laced shoes that were puffy like two suede bladders.

Once I had changed my clothes I walked in no direction. At

one point I caught sight of my face in a window, and I saw that my features were darker and longer than they had been when I had last seen my face in Parry's bathroom the night before.

In a handy shop I located English cider with an easy-to-open-lid. Waiting to cross the road again I aimed for a pigeon-bedecked public statue where my hostilities would take on a different light. Union Street lay before me and I sat down and waited. The noise of the day had become nothing more than a chiding murmur nearby. Beyond the roofs I could see the rusted green teacup of Cowdray Hall. A cat approached from nowhere and I enticed it over for a stroke. I recalled the list of names that Liska and I had for the day when we would get a cat, and I drank for them all:

> Our shortlist of cat names : Sholto, Rees, Zonabend,
> Monkswell, Batto, Bekko, Scatto, Tatto, Bernico, Chip,
> Baddeley, Relictus, Hubler, Dorcas, Clonfert, Chester,
> Ab, Osgot, Domingo, Chesapeake, Ace, Belvin,
> Dolphus, Cluke, Kennis, Mord, Jarveena, Poke, Noyce,
> Athers, Shehleypea, Langton, Earl, Pads and Biscuit.

I drank slowly and felt good. The cat sniffed at the cider bottle and went on its way, and I waited there as the morning ended, and the people started lunch.

Would I have liked to have seen myself at the bottom of the sea? The answer was no — I still preferred the world above. Tallowy pieces of food sat in wet newspaper beneath the bench. I looked down my trouser leg to a puddle and mulled on the amusing consequences of my escape from death. The centre of the puddle was a dark patch where the truth of the world was side-tracked into a mysterious swirl. In the puddle I saw the reflection of an aeroplane passing until someone walked through and disturbed the water. The image of the sky was shattered and a skateboarder crashed in the wave and whooped with glee. When the skateboarder had gone something of the same old absolute settled on the puddle. My second-hand shoes were fat and comic. They were not even comfortable. Liska was a shade of bone held in check by the material of her dress. She raised an arm and turned on her side. A current moved her until she was standing upright, a mild undulation in the flow. Afternoon depressed the city so much that for a minute its entire sound was reduced to one train horn. Liska would like me in these shoes, I thought. She would like the fat brown Saharan leather and the rainbow-coloured laces.

I looked at the statue above me — a man on horse. A newspaper blew up and wiped the horse's leg, threatening to fly before the traffic. Cars leeched along Union Street — across the seabed and through the pockets at the bottom of the lagoon. The newspaper blew into the air, geed up by the lacustrian bubbles of a row of piled up litter. As the paper landed before me its message became obvious. A flick of sunshine illuminated a picture of Liska. Another piece of paper showed the charred remains of what I guessed were Liska's paintings, and the text informed me that her works were under attack. I felt a sickening desire to laugh. The exhalation of righteousness, like a burp from the throat, made me dizzy as I took the paper in my hand and unfolded it, shaking off the water.

According to the newspaper Liska's works had been separated the day after I had left our flat and, most fatefully of all, two out of the 58 had already been spotted by other artists and destroyed. Several of the remaining paintings had changed hands following Liska's death, and other works of hers had surfaced both in Aberdeen and in London. The puddle quivered and I read the newspaper closely until a second later, the cathode ray tube on the end of my eye-stalk printed the following words in my mind — the words of Joseph Gram — quoted after these posthumous attacks on Liska's work:

WE CALL ON ALL ARTISTS NEVER TO SHOW YOUR WORK! he had said.

I sat on a bench and people came and went. The picture of Liska in the paper was the dearest thing I had ever seen and I couldn't help returning to it. The revolution continued profitably around me. Every working man and woman in Aberdeen stammered forth and I walked repeatedly around the statue, drinking until the cider was done. Finally, a hand clapped my shoulder, a human touch. The exceeding happiness of my situation was brought to life when I saw that it was Parry in his traffic warden costume.

"Good afternoon," he said.

Parry had crossed the road — a brave man in this day and age. He eyed me up and down but his outthought was stopped at the gate of his mouth and he eventually spluttered, "Those clothes are daft!"

I agreed and stared at him, planet-struck drifter that I now was.

"I have to get back now," he said.

"Do you?" I said and Parry stepped away.

"Yes," he said, "I've got to go back to work."

In my new clothes I had a trampy feeling. One morning on the streets and I had developed disruptive tendencies. "I'll leave tomorrow," I said. "But it would be good to stay again."

Parry cocked his head. "It's OK," he said. "I'll give your regards to the others. They've been asking all about you."

"Shit those others," I said. "And don't tell them that you saw me."

Parry looked surprised as he walked away but I waved to let him know that I was just drunk.

"See you later," said Parry from a safe distance.

I bowed my head as Parry drifted towards the traffic where he would lose himself again. The artistic validity of this parish is not helped by people having to go to work, I thought, just as they once had to go to school — and so I shall not follow him — instead I shall go and browse the gallerias.

34.

■ Wandering out of Aberdeen city centre and refreshed by cider, it so happened that I was pleased as hell with myself until I was struck by my past and reminded once more of my enormous debt to Liska. Here is the story:

Staying in Aberdeen like this I could not sit still, and although without direction it appeared that I may end up anywhere, I could not resist the magnetism of the galleries. It was only a matter of time therefore before I jumped on a bus and arrived back on Deeside outside the Myrtle Gallery, where I stopped before the painting by Liska which they had displayed in their window.

"This is all wrong," I said, and I dropped my cider on the ground. "Liska wanted all of her pictures to be shown together, if at all. She never gave anybody the permission to show her shit like this."

Of course I knew the painting well. An image of the sea — a silver body of water and a fragile hand of clouds that looked like petals — a tangle of ribbons burned by traces of fire made the sun — the result being an odd mixture of purity and error, as if she had painted it with her thumbs. The painting was essential Liska, and I recognised it easily. The painting was in Liska's typical style. The oil paint had been mixed to the density of putty and then thinned out with her hand, and the picture had been completed with a soldering iron with which she scratched the final outline. Liska's spirit was like a sensitive seismographic machine. This was a burning bright seascape with the sun red like torn lips, and underneath it was a card:

Liska Final Works

Final Works? Was that more wordplay?

I remembered the painting because it had hung in our studio for half a year. In my memory Liska and I were both hard at work, mixing damar and mastic on our electric stove, stirring until they combined completely. We cooled the mixture and poured it into a bottle — and that was what she'd use to get her splashing effect.

Outside the Myrtle Gallery I was hypnotised by Liska's seascape but angry that it was here before me on a richly varnished stand. Liska had painted the sea so many times but that wasn't the point — already her collection had broken apart without her permission.

I heard feet crunching on the gravel but I didn't turn to look. All I knew was that I was not alone and that some other people were approaching from the main road. I saw them as they joined me at the gallery window — a young couple — the very people who could afford an oil painting like this. My jaw locked as the man who was looking at Liska's painting said to his partner,

"The whole of her career in an image that seems to displace all her other pictures at the same time."

The man's words were effortless and he threw them over his shoulder towards the North Deeside Road, where they dispersed like mercury in the deep sea of the traffic. The man's explanation pinched me, the high and dry of his critique. On a tablet of cardboard on the gallery door was a message advertising that the premises were modestly stocked with the work of Liska.

Set you back a good few months that will.

A voice spoke to me — one of the many menaces of the mind.

cf. Liska : *Untitled 34 of 58* Signed and numbered and dated on the reverse with a key to its positioning. Oil and enamel on canvas.

As artists, Liska and I were, in truth, frightened by the galleries. The galleries were one of many nerve-racking corners where cruel dissections awaited us — and seeing Liska's paintings like this was a disaster. There were memories in seeing Liska's picture in the window of the Myrtle Gallery, but nothing I could salvage. I tried to return to normal — backed by the energising sound of cars moving to the next dark red light on the North Deeside Road but instead my thoughts groped shadily for that memory of my love. A flock of tiny birds rushed overhead and the perspective of that outdoor scene extended to a generality of cars, houses and treetops — and Liska's painting shone. It was an ability she had — the most perverse attainment in art today — to show light in every form.

I stopped as if I'd forgotten something. The couple at the window were engrossed in conversation. I glanced over my shoulder and it was this action that indicated to me I was about to do something inappropriate. It was like being afforded a glimpse of another person. I should have been walking back to Parry's flat or going for a drink, or applying for a job as a traffic warden — but instead I returned to the Myrtle Gallery and stopped under the detested arch that braced its door. My thoughts, impulses and desires were overlapping, like shifting mud closing up a hole.

I pulled the lever door of the art gallery and entered. Within, everything was solitary, dehumanised and expensive. The gallery was stocked with miniature metal statuary and brilliantly lit clay pots — reality stylised in the imagination of the over-priced. The two ladies working in the gallery wore chunky beads and held pens like mechanical props — and I ignored them by staring hard at the art, street loafer that I was. Underneath Liska's first canvas was a tacked square of card indicating the price of X thousand. Next to the price were hyperbolic statements indicating that Liska was an outstanding young painter who had produced 58 paintings, all of which were untitled.

It was Liska's desire that the 58 paintings be exhibited as one, said the card, but unfortunately this has not been possible post her dying.

The printed card on the wall pretended to quote Liska and said the paintings had 'come about through sleep deprivation', which was a surprise because I had never thought of Liska's insomnia as a conscious tactic. When I read the card again, I was sure that Liska could never have said that. Perhaps it was journalistic fantasy, perhaps indignation at the lack of information available.

I was the only visitor in the gallery and my hand was in my pocket, gripping one of Parry's pens which felt tough and sharp. In Liska's picture there could have been a cat's face or a tree, a fruit or a star constellation. All of these things were in the picture and yet it was still in its basic form a tangle of clouds and shadows. I pressed my finger into the nib of the pen and wondered if I could use it to streak a rip from one corner of Liska's canvas to the other. There were three paintings by Liska in the gallery, all in the consummate mildness of the exhibition space, and I looked at them each in turn and wondered how best to destroy them. With the two paintings on the wall and the one in the window, and only the two baubled ladies of art to prevent me, I felt that my chances were good. The most mild, peaceful feelings crossed my mind.

I looked over my shoulder. There was a camera in the gallery roof and the black nozzle of its lens pointed at me. I looked into the camera and was caught forever. The waves in Liska's oil painting were dark, alert like Liska's own wildest dreams. I moved towards the nearest picture and bent closer for examination.

If I am fast, I thought, I can destroy these paintings and I might get away with it. I can destroy the pictures as per Liska's wish and get back to Parry's and hide out.

I prepared to attack, admiring my clenched hand and pointing the pen at its target, but once more I failed to act. Being in the gallery was different from being on the ferry, but still I paused, as if suffering from stage-fright.

35

☐   All of which struck me as strange as I stood, in the Myrtle Gallery in Aberdeen, waiting for the impetus to destroy three of Liska's pictures.

I'd forgotten everything. I wasn't a painter any more, just fast becoming another variety of social nonentity. I didn't feel as careful as I might have been, having drunk alcohol for lunch, and the frames of Liska's pictures, gilded by the spotlighting, winked at me and I wobbled, unable to find anything on which to steady myself.

It had all gone wrong for Liska. Until I saw those pictures I'd hoped that what was left of her work would remain together as she wished, but it had all gone wrong and it felt as if nothing she had said had impressed itself on anybody.

No matter. Liska's paintings dominated the room with their partially burnt greys and reds. What people liked about the pictures, I knew, was that when you moved closer to them all sorts of items became visible, so although the overall picture appeared to be abstract, at a much finer level, a richer language was available. This richer language included the sea, boats, flowers and bottles, and other of Liska's favourites, but there was much more, as in a picture of the tree of life, which aimed to encompass every plant and animal within it, and even portraits.

The gallery ladies twisted their pens on the catalogues, seeming to enjoy something private. I, on the other hand, looked at the security eye and swayed in time with the room. A puffy leather chair in the corner was beating like a black heart. A dull sheet of metal had been decorated with a torn flag, itself blackened and burned and labelled:

Shona Gelding : *Tribute to an American Indian* (1994)

People are so tenacious, I thought. They can't let anything be. Liska hadn't sold a single painting when she'd been alive and had diligently destroyed all of the ones that had been exhibited. She never said why her 58 surviving pictures should remain together and she never said why none of them were for sale. Liska didn't like it when people used artwork as props. What was important to her was that her work should never end up in the dump of a city gallery, along with everybody else's commercial compositions.

I pressed my finger into my pen. Outside, the couple in their coats gazed with faint smiles at the oil painting by Liska in the window. Both he and she had put on heavy-framed spectacles. Nearby, and above the River Dee, the trees suffered their early evening emptiness.

"Hello," said the art seller in my ear.

A discreet woman with clasped hands, she would have mocked anything you offered her.

"We've had these for two days," she said. "They're new to us."

I looked into the seller's face. The genetic difference in class between her and me was radical enough to ensure that she was two inches taller than I was.

"You know they're all by Liska," she said.

I nodded. The seller knew that I owned no art, but she kept a cheerful face as she folded her arms and placed the baubles in the custody of her breasts.

"I'm glad to see people are at least here to view her work," she said, and I thought the word 'yes' might do as an answer to her statement. My finger pressed into the backbone of Parry's pen as I felt an incredible energy stir in me. The pen would tear these pictures of Liska's to pieces when the art seller sat down again.

"Do you know the work of Liska?" asked the art seller in that moment.

I shook my head.

"There's a sketch here of a flower," said the art seller as she opened a folder. "It was taken from her notebooks. It's going to be very collectible."

I was appalled that a sketch had been taken from the flat and I was pretty sure who was behind it. The sketch was private and always had been, and as I presented my rigid profile to it, I wondered where they could have dug it out from.

"Why do you have this here?" I asked.

"It's of interest," said the baubled gallery worker.

"It's of more interest to Liska," I said.

I almost felt like snatching the picture and making a run for it.

"What do you mean it's of interest to Liska?" she asked.

"A composer of music doesn't fling herself into ecstasy at a musical performance," I said.

The art seller stared long and hard, unsure what I was suggesting. Seeing that I was in earnest, she said nothing, merely let out a brittle chuckle and returned to her desk.

I wasn't angry that Liska's work was on show — but I'd something else in mind — my many memories. These were my memories of Liska, now dead in the North Sea without me. Liska could have moved at any moment, lifted a hand up from the sea bed and clicked her fingers slowly — and that crackling from the bottom of the sea shelf would have been enough to cause a calamity. I realised how dangerous it was in here. Liska could destroy this building from the dark vault of the deep.

"I used to be frightened of flowers when I was a child," said Liska, "especially orchids. You could see them in the winter gardens and I used to be scared of them whenever I came up close."

The flower in Liska's sketch had demonstrated this threatening quality. The petals of the orchid led the viewer to its centre where their attention was taken with something near impossible, like an eye looking back. The orchid in the sketch was, therefore, a sharp-eyed plant, sensing the viewer was there. Having seen that sketch again, I remembered many flowers and many mornings in the hothouse, so much so that the task in hand was somewhat blanked out, or obscured.

It's time to destroy these three paintings, I thought as another illuminating moment of suffering passed me by in the sudden vertigo of my new life without Liska.

Liska had said it — my paintings should be exhibited at the same time — if they're ever separated then they'll be destroyed.

Statement and fulfilment. Everything Liska had feared about the art game had come to pass and now she was floating, somewhat surreal before my eyes, about to witness my greatest action in her defence.

36

◼   People destroy works of art for a variety of reasons. Sometimes they believe that a work of art is valued by other people more than they are. Others have had political motives.

> cf. Paul Kelleher : *The Destruction of the Statue of Margaret Thatcher Abortively with a Cricket Bat and then with a Metal Pole* (2002) Criminal Damage on marble, three month sentence.

Sometimes a mania is a personal fixation that carries itself to a violent conclusion, much like a murder — and sometimes it's an accident — as in the case of Heery the Hippie of Multiple Solitude who built a twenty foot driftwood Ossian, which blew away into the porridge of the North Sea.

Then there was the time that Nelson Rockefeller commissioned Diego Rivera to paint a mural for him. This was going very well until Rivera's finished work was found to feature an image of Lenin and the scene was pulverised. Rockefeller just wouldn't have it and the art had to be annihilated.

Sometimes, and for reasons postmoydern, the destruction of the work can be integral to the work itself. I think of David Mach's matchstick bust of R.L. Stevenson, which several of us saw go up in flames in a Scottish town, circa 2001.

Liska interrupted. "The sale of art doesn't destroy the artist. It only destroys the art — surely?"

> cf. Clementine Ogilvy Spencer-Churchill : *Destruction of Graham Sutherland's Portrait of Winston Churchill* (1954) oil on canvas, in ribbons, on fire.

Liska waited for me to answer, but I never did. Destroying art was proving difficult, like suicide had been. I was still not doing anything, and the art seller was watching me, her arms folded in the purple of a cardigan.

I looked at Liska's painting. The work was technical — a representation of the sea but stuffed with finer details that in places even spelled words.

Once I've destroyed the pictures, I thought, I'll run and hide. Once hidden, I thought, I can only hope that art vandalism is low on the agendas of the authorities.

It was time for my crime to take place — but I waited.

The couple at the window were looking into the gallery through those false spectacles. The gentleman held his professional leather case against his chest and gazed right at me. I held my pen like a sword and felt the nib that I would use to cut the canvas. Then I took several steps back.

There is nothing that anybody can do to stop me, I thought — and the first thing I did, the action by which I raised my arm to the correct height — was to pretend to scratch my head.

37

☐   The Myrtle Gallery in Aberdeen is advertised by propaganda unequalled hitherto in its repugnance. Invitations are sent and the beasts respond. Wine is served before the derivatively produced art-for-sale, and names from the fashion-hat are circulated. The business of hagiography is important. Backers like to know they are supporting saints, should any of that holiness rub off on them. Cubist monochrome may clash with the collage elements of the contemporary concept, and the art of today may be disappointingly inward looking, but it can always be talked up a little further.

> cf. Andres Serrano : *How to Push the Limits of Acceptability with Urine* (1987) Cibachrome in artist's frame, 40 x 60 inches of pee.

I paused before the paintings. I was paused before them only a second ago and I was paused before them at the start of the story. I'm paused before the paintings all of the time — me and eternal return — and I ask myself why the art world is all so gimmicky, glamorous, witty and nerve-shudderingly arty.

It's always happening. I'm proof of the retention of that moment which stops the world and can only start again from the place I left it. My pen was held fast in my hand, but maybe, I thought, my shoes would be better?

Yes, that's a point. I might be able to kick the paintings to pieces more effectively with my shoes — or my fingernails — or my hands — or my teeth — or —

For my lack of action, I blamed the tremendous tension of my grief, but that was no excuse. Like on the ferry, I couldn't do it — that was all. Liska's works had been split up, yes — and she was making money for the first time — so perhaps I should at least stay and witness, I figured. The young couple were walking through the door, rubbing the leafless branches of their hands in anticipation. Neither of this young couple would stop me in my act. Not him — he seemed too shy, and not her — she looked like a page of calculus, pointed and neat.

The camera lens crossed the room. As the couple neared to look at Liska's pictures, I took another look at the spectacles they wore. Their spectacles, with their overly large and plastic black frames, made the couple look like puppets.

I pretended to look at a nearby picture and gripped my pen but my path to the art was suddenly blocked. The young couple with the black spectacles stepped in front of me and stood before Liska's pictures like they were taking position to shoot something.

Indeed, the young couple had guns. I could tell from the way they stood at first — the way the pause button came off when they took up their positions. When the young couple unbuttoned their coats and opened their bags it looked to me like they were breathing fire from their arms. First there was a pulse of expanding air and in it an eruption of smoke, and hurtling particles as fire shot between the young couples' bodies and the wall. I protected my face with my arms against the red and blue flames but as the fire hit the paintings, the sound was of the city itself — like a train going through the room — or an explosion. Fire flowed in a jet, up the gallery wall, and in seconds, Liska's paintings barely existed. With two decisive steps, the young man had pulled Liska's third painting out of the window of the gallery and tossed it on the floor, where they similarly torched it. Another rack of flame and I protected my face, and in that second the water sprinkler began and a ridiculous alarm made a blooping noise from the back of the gallery. The two art sellers backed off, shouting. I was drenched in water and Liska's paintings had vanished.

The couple turned to look at me. Their thick spectacles were safety glasses and oil dripped from the nozzles of their home-made flame guns. With their hair flattened by water from the sprinklers, the couple looked their real age — approximately 21. The young couple held two flame-throwers, each had a thick metal pipe, covered in shabby black marks, and as quickly as they had acted, they folded their weapons into two pieces and readied to leave.

It occurred to me then that these people had acted on Liska's own conscience, and what a remarkable thing that was. I would have liked to have spoken to the young couple if I had been able to open my mouth. The truth was that I couldn't open my mouth for anything other than the most basic monkey noises.

The young couple left the gallery and pulled on woollen hats. They left me with the shreds of Liska's beautiful images, standing in the sprinkler system and listening to the prudent bloop of the building's alarm.

Front view of a wet figure —. surprise in his expression — a violent beating in his heart — an anguished man, sprinkled in water from the roof.

I broke my pose. Safety first, you see. I didn't want to be in the gallery when the cops arrived, and so, like a normal person leaving an art show, I walked to the door and looked back one more time. The frames of Liska's pictures had survived the assault, but the heat had scorched the wall where they hung. As for what was left, there were a few snatches — a moment of colour but no shape.

That's what I like in my artists, I thought as I shut the door and joined the crowd of onlookers. Closure.

38

■   Outside the Myrtle Gallery bystanders caught the mood of the scene. At the bus stop, hens with king-size cigarettes were clucking. Two mums with prams had pulled to a stop and were looking gingerly towards the building. Chivalrously, a young man in a suit ran across the gravel and into the gallery. Liska's pictures had been reabsorbed into the private realm, where only she would know them, and now the gallery needed emergency cataloguists and critics. Most of all, journalists would have to be rushed in.

I walked towards the North Deeside Road, dripping water. Suicide was never going to happen for me, even though blackness still pervaded my days. The comedy of life was too good to miss. The only fierce impulse that had risen within me in days had been the one to destroy those paintings, and I'd been unable to act. I'd wanted to do it but someone else had done it for me.

This was Scary Me replaced by Happy Me.

Scary Me	Happy Me
"I'm pleased sir. We've issued more than 20 tickets today."	"I'm pleased with my novel. It's going very well."
"I want to be an artist."	"I want to be a dragon."
"What kind of sandwich do you want?"	"Tell me your Buddhic prophecies."
"How dare you disagree?"	"Of course I'm wrong."

I looked along the road but the young couple with the flame-throwers had departed. Vehicles belted out towards the satellite towns and there I stood and dripped. The enormous ox of a road-transporter ran past me, and the turbulence rocked me from side to side. Although the vibrations of the vehicles rattled my head, I could still think clearly. This time I resolved that the next chance I got to act, I would.

As readers whom I'm sure share with me the most acute sensitivity to a fellow being's mental discomfort, you will not have failed to have been touched by this most moving of episodes. It is, I think I am right in saying, the first time since Mrs Winston Churchill destroyed Sutherland's portrait of her husband, that a member of the public has evinced clear signs of mental anguish by taking aggression out on a painting.

I walked back to the city as the roadway quietened for the night. Head down, I travelled the carpet of paving stones, past shops with increasingly illegible names, and back to Aberdeen. I was damp and my legs were cold where my trousers had stuck.

Parry let me into his house but said nothing, and then he went out for the evening, leaving me in a sulk. On the coffee table was the only sign of upset, an empty bottle of wine from the night before and a dark cup of coffee from the morning. The television was speaking patiently to itself and I removed my trousers and crumpled them. I took off my shirt and held it up.

All shall be flat and without a crease, I thought. Tomorrow all will be new and I will start again.

39

☐   In one respect the trip to the gallery had been a success, and I settled at the window of Parry's flat to reflect. Rosemount was dark. On the opposite building, I had the red-lighted spike of a mobile phone mast for a view and the sound of a police siren completed the scene. Parry's stock of alcohol was available and I assumed that I had rights and helped myself.

I looked across the city from Parry's window — the end of the story, I might have thought. I drank a bottle of wine and fell asleep for several hours, waking up at the very moment I heard Liska's name mentioned on the television. Awake and focussed, I knew what was going on.

I was not disappointed.

Liska was now a minor item on the news — and there had been a day of it.

Above the spectre of the newsreader there was a picture of Liska on the television. I listened as the newsreader said that, in all, four people were in custody.

A weakness took over. My stomach revolted and imaginary spikes dug in. The resulting pain was sudden. It wasn't the picture of Liska that did it, but the police gravely announcing that a total of ten paintings had been destroyed by combinations of acid, fire and swords.

They came organised for the destruction, said the deep, feeling voice of the reporter, *and police have linked this attack with similar attacks elsewhere. We now know that paintings by Liska were vandalised both north and south of the border, and that guards have been placed on all surviving works.*

The pictures flashed up in Omnicolor. I recognised Liska's work, but when I saw the state of it I was surprised. One person had even put his painting by Liska in a cage, which seemed tantamount to putting her in a cage.

Estimates say that up to a third of Liska's work may have been destroyed. In the most serious of these attacks, art collector Frank Capt was beaten in his house last night while he attempted to halt the destruction of the piece known as No. 3.

No. 3 was displayed. I wiped my face and prepared for the strange fright of revisiting my past. The image returned — Liska painting this very picture, using our neighbour's tomato plant as a model. Brief moments of colours (she said), a part of a leaf, not a whole leaf, (she said).

As *No. 3* faded into the background, an art critic with putty for arms appeared on the television screen and explained that Liska had wanted all her works to be exhibited in one place, but that they'd been split up in the days after her death.

I can only assume art purists have carried out these attacks, said the critic. *Given that most work by Liska is either not on display or held by private collectors such a plan is certainly going to fail. It's very interesting though,* he said, *to see an artist's wishes being carried out like this. I'd warn people who own any of Liska's work to remove them to somewhere safe.*

I placed a fresh bottle of wine to my lips. The news told of Liska and how she had worked. It mentioned the North Sea where she had disappeared and there was a flash of a North Sea ferry, and the gallery where I had been.

I wondered if Anna Lunken's house had been attacked?

When the news returned to the usual mendacity of war and economic growth, I lay down and waited for Parry to come in. When he did return, he was very excited. He'd been in the bar with his crowd and they'd all been talking about Liska too.

"Dead artists are correct in pointing out that what is said in favour of their work does not relativise the fact of their works having being bought and sold constantly after their lives have finished," he said, seemingly sober despite being plastered drunk. "The monetary value of paintings by dead artists is not intended to apply a value but places the quality of the work in a far sharper light," he said. "Academia's bondage to the dead has never helped — merely destroyed the absolute distinction between art and the possibility of it becoming money."

I nodded.

"It's sad," he said. "Liska's paintings are going to be indefinitely transferred from room to room in exchange for money for the rest of their lives. It's not what she wanted. I can see that now."

> cf. Deborah Shophet : *Chapter 19 of My Poor Life* (1985) Mannequin split into 12 pieces, polyester, wood, paint.

Parry was correct but what was so exciting was that people had taken Liska's notions far enough to attack galleries. I didn't complain. It's not enough that an artist should make art. They've got to be bent over in a gallery with their pants down before they're properly called an artist these days. Destroying Liska's work struck me as a positive action in a world that seemed far too tied to one general tendency. Interest in art was either commercial or snobbish and neither were satisfactory. Parry and I shared the wine, and I listened as he told me how a new impasse had been reached in the decadent society. Smokey-faced gallery owners, silver-suited investors, and all the shit and smack of the media — everyone was horsing loudly about how awful it was, while anticipating what was going to happen next, all in an effort to ramp up interest, prices and reputations.

"Liska was different," he said, and I told Parry about the two young art-breakers and how they had been dressed as caricatures of the class they were criticising — and I wondered if I would recognise them again if I saw them.

"You're a hero," said Parry — and that made me sit up and take notice. In the absence of Liska I might be the next target.

Like the peaking of a sickness, Liska was returning to me. Although she'd been long washed to the mud of the Baltic, I felt better knowing that at any time, there was going to be another reminder of Liska, and that I was going to be getting a coarse kick in the throat, if not from her, then from somebody nearer to home. I felt ready for it.

▉   When the traffic jammed and slowed to the speed of seashells and blocked the side roads that fed the city centre, the traffic wardens moved in, floating between windscreens and attaching tickets. They were good at their jobs — as were the police. I knew that I'd been captured on the gallery video so what could I expect?

SCENE: Police Station

"I want to know who that is!" says the cop gaffer, thrusting his finger on the screen. "I want him on my desk on Monday morning!"

"That's Guy Poynting," says somebody. "He's definitely involved in this business, and in deep."

"Who the hell is Guy Poynting?" asks the gaffer.

"The man that used to be Liska's boyfriend!"

"The artist!"

"That's it. And the best part is this. Do you know that he disappeared in Aberdeen several days ago?"

"Disappeared?"

"That's right. He was questioned but nobody saw him again after that."

Rapt with attention the hopeful detectives peer for more detail of the figure on screen.

"That's him. I'm sure that's him! They say that he killed her!"

"Killed her?"

The video frame is released, one stop at a time. From the grimed up pixels of the image, two flames materialise and burst across the room from the young couple. There is a flash and the fire charges into the wall where the paintings are hanging.

"Not bad firepower," says the detective — and he dashes out of the video suite to run upstairs and tell King Kong the news.

SCENE: Upstairs at the Nick

All the moustaches are delighted with the news.

"A dead cert, you'd say. There's bound to be a link. I'll stake my badge on it."

"Yep — there's no such thing as coincidence," says the superintendent, and he pulls out a clipboard and scratches his tits.

Their next move was to track me down. I didn't know the police could do this but they are part spirit and part human. The police see through anything and find people easily, because they can use remote viewing techniques and other visionary tools.

It was like the television shop window I ran past while that first cop was chasing me. It hit me — all those screens — about twenty of them — reflecting the mob reflexes of the viewers — twenty screens and all with the same image. If the homogeneity is going to be that obvious, I thought, it really is a very good time for me to try once again to kill myself.

> cf. Douglas Gordon : *Predictable Incidents in Unfamiliar Surroundings* (2003) The slowing of classic film. TV time drags time and again. The same scream and the same screen kiss.

Poor policeman. One moment you're thinking of your dinner and the next you're chasing artists up and down the outlandish ramps of an indoor shopping centre. You don't even know why you're chasing them, half the time. You have your orders and you follow them.

I tried to differentiate between the people and the more static solid objects in my way as I left the shopping centre. I saw a gap in the traffic and thought I'd take it — and on the other side of the road I banged right into a sculpture, spun away from it and carried on down the pavement.

> cf. Gertrude Punter : *Statuesque* (2004) Public street art. It may have been a sculpture. Perhaps it was just a girl with flowers, standing very still.

People looked unfavourably on me as I frustrated the attempts of several hundred pigeons to slow me down. When I ran past security guards and other traffic wardens, they seemed to be in on it too — at least they put their fingers to their ears, which meant that they were receiving messages. The public stared with faces like beef.

I realised I had lost the policeman for now, but that this being a top-heavy authoritarian police state, I knew would be caught in no time. Underneath the granite and glass offices, I looked into the crowd for somewhere to start again, and I was about to dash for the only place I knew, Parry's flat, when a voice shouted from behind me.

"Stop there Guy!" said the voice, and, as if the instruction had come from my own mind, I did.

A small young man puffed up beside me.

"Man, I've caught you," he said, loud words from sore lungs.

This was Paul Raytheon — the star of the story — struggling with a substantial shoulder bag — trying to slow me down while readjusting large spectacles. Like me, you may not immediately recognise Paul Raytheon — even though we have already met him.

"Are you following me?" I asked, and there was much nodding from the small guy. His anorak made him look like a party political canvasser and he dropped his shoulder bag where it planted itself on the pavement. He stood with his hands on his knees and deep-breathed.

"I saw you running," he said, and he pointed towards the West End, up the Queen's Road. "Come with me. I know somewhere safe."

This is good, I thought. My friend pulled at his anorak and heaved his bag up before he walked again.

"Who are you?" I asked.

My new friend wore glasses which loaned him a fragility that was comforting and non-threatening. His beard curved neatly to a stop beneath his chin and he offered me his hand.

"Paul Raytheon," he said, "Ottawa." He grabbed my hand and shook it.

"Do you think the police will come?" I asked Paul Raytheon, and the anorak rustled.

"Oh yeah," he said. "We'll just have to get moving."

"Why did you follow me?" I asked.

"For art," he said, and pointed up the avenue. "This way."

We headed west, to where a lofty vista of terraced houses formed a separate town, a wealthy suburban sprawl called Rubislaw.

"I'm taking you to our place," said Paul Raytheon. A moment later a police car passed, cruising at sinister speed, a bitter white colour in the traffic. The police car chilled the street with its promise of violence and scared me so much that my neck froze.

"Take it easy and don't look at it," said Paul Raytheon, his hand still on his heavy bag.

The police car passed and was gone — an exciting interlude. Paul Raytheon smiled and pointed to the high end of the city.

"We gotta lay low," he said.

I said nothing — I was already laying low.

I kept my head down and thought about Liska. I could see her — she was handling old pieces of iron, rubbing her palms on her seabed treasures. Liska was sculpting among the frayed debris of the deep. Why would she be sculpting at the bottom of the sea when sculpture is such an earthly pastime? I don't know. Who can appreciate art in that void — and with neither air nor light? I didn't know that either, but as I walked, Liska harried through the mud and rock at the bottom of the sea, like a familiar spirit, moving her sculptured collections in and out of position. She could see me through the cold slush of the water, and I gaped in wonder. When she saw me looking back at her, Liska pulled the darkness over the mouth of her cave and vanished.

Soon, Paul Raytheon walked up a gravel drive towards a grossly gabled granite house and stuck his key in a chipped wooden side door, pushing it open enough to squeeze himself through. The house was so large that it must have had at least three entrances.

"Tradesperson's entrance," he said, and I followed him into the dark.

I wondered if this was the mighty studio that Mr Sharma had talked about. A green stain to the darkness shone around the features of Paul Raytheon's face and as my eyes adjusted to the scene, I began to make out a mural that covered the whole area. It made me wonder again whether mural art shouldn't be given its own unsaleable category — a genre dedicated to all the art that won't fit into the aristocratic white spaces of our arcades. There were faces and scenes, but mostly the walls were embosomed with captions like:

ART FOR ART'S SAKE
SURRENDER DOROTHY
DUCHAMP OUR CHAMP

Paul Raytheon gripped the door at the top of the stairs and with a kick, let us in to a section of the house that had been converted into artists' living quarters. The third door down was his and with a smile he installed me within it. I kicked away my shoes and sat to rest on the beige urbanity of his bed.

Paul Raytheon's room was a stack of paper. Carpet space was retained, bed space was retained, and computer gear was organised to the last detail. There was a tiny window which allowed grey light to enter, and as I rested my head on the feather pillows, Paul Raytheon picked up my shoes and asked if everything was all right. Raytheon's voice was so loud I was too scared to say anything. I smiled and the lavender strips of his lips smiled back.

"I'll be back when I've told the others," he said and he smiled proudly and turned away.

"Duchamp," I said after him. "Who likes Duchamp?"

Paul Raytheon came all the way back to the bed to tell me. He was in no doubt of his answer.

"Everybody," he said. "Everybody likes Duchamp. The artist is a hypocrite, who first takes himself in with the sound of his own voice. And that's why everybody likes Duchamp."

41

☐   I rested, gazing at the ceiling. I had been reminded of Duchamp — the genius of him. Duchamp had been, in my opinion, not just a lord of art, glib, condescending and effortlessly virtuoso — but a great poet, a demonic. Liska had been a huge admirer of his work and his stance, although we had never been able to figure out how he had come about his immense intellectual confidence. How else, if not by some Faustian pact?

Perhaps his madness was a clue.

All Duchamp's demonic brilliance was compensation for the loss of reality he felt. For Duchamp, art had been mutilated when it had been forced into service as the stuff of bourjoissy pleasure. This traumatic loss of continuity must have pushed open an already willing door into his obsessive genius — and I think that's why Duchamp appealed to Liska — he was the first of us to realise the falsity of the process and the first to subvert it. Whether we know it or not, all our ideas and ironies were the crumbs from Duchamp's table, the fallout from his thoughts and actions, every one of which must have been an unholy blow against the world-wide forces of aestheticism.

Nobody else knew what art was for — but they kept on asking Duchamp! — which must have made him madder yet. So Duchamp began to wonder when it was that art became art. Liska argued that a work of art was destroyed when it was sold — that it ceased at that point. This was opposed to the art purchasing view that attributed value to a work of art at the point of purchase, and shifted a certain amount of semantic complexity into place to demonstrate this new discriminate category.

Words = Value as in £1000 per 'excellent!'

Artists may appear anti-social but all of them would buck their hams to get on in the art market while still aware that at times, they might as well be selling plates of lasagne.

> cf. Joseph Beuys : *The Rembrandt of Lasagne* (1983) Oil paint, acrylic paint, paper collage, glitter, polyester resin, map pins, cooked Italianate tomato and mozzarella lasagne on linen.

Artists, Duchamp realised, have a terrible itch for the praise of fools — and was he not right?

42

■   When I woke, the light from Paul Raytheon's small window had announced another bad-luck day. I hadn't wanted to go to sleep but with nothing to do I had drifted back to unconsciousness. Liska was close. About this time each day she floated up to breathe. Her bones were like cork in the waves and nothing would keep them down. I was in Paul Raytheon's bed and everything was unfamiliar.

Paul Raytheon was moving outside — he was on the telephone. He must have been talking about me because my ears hurt. I wished that Paul Raytheon didn't know who I was, but my insomnolent ears heard differently. My face had been recognised — my head had been spotted, and I could hear him on the phone, and he was letting everybody know that I was there.

Comfortable in Paul Raytheon's bed, I tried to approach the blackness under the covers, but in that blackness was where Liska was at her strongest, obliging me to talk. Liska would never sleep again. She spent every day wading through the mud, couched in a belt of dead sand, a napping fifty-foot bank of sludge in which heavy-eyed sea pods watched her.

I heard Paul Raytheon approach the bedroom door. He was talking art, of course. "I'm working on a piece," I heard Paul Raytheon say. "Dark — I guess —" A pause and Paul Raytheon spoke again "— on art and war — on wear and tear. The self in —"

I had heard enough of that.

I suffered in Paul Raytheon's bedroom while outside, narcissism declared war on culture. I'd seen artists like him before. They made expeditions against every tactic that they imagined thwarting them.

cf. Toby Trockel : *My Pain is More Interesting Than Yours*
(1996) Compact Disc with the artist's voice (screaming)
[running time approx 15 min.], light bulb, sound organ
kit. The light bulb reacts to the frequency of the voice
on the CD.

I felt squeamish as I watched a brisk procession of remembrances
that ended on the back of a ferry boat — a long time ago. The boat
was turning in the water, a ghost ship. Liska fell like an angel making
her last dive. I was crying — mouth open in horror, there was no
getting away from it. A wild hunt on the sea but Liska's body has
sunk and will never be found.

I pulled the covers up and Liska poked her head out of her
sub-Baltic trough, while fingers of seaweed hung in the gloom. I
concentrated on Paul Raytheon's voice.

"All I'm doing is manipulating distance," said Paul Raytheon.

The bedroom door opened and the anoraks that hung there
whispered — and then Paul Raytheon walked away and I heard him
saying his enthusiastic Canadian goodbyes on the phone. I listened
to hear if Paul Raytheon would say my name, but heard nothing
— just the deep North Atlantic clamber of his saying 'Hello!' to
another caller.

I looked around for my shoes. While Paul Raytheon's shoes were
parked like barges at the cupboard door, mine were nowhere to be
seen. My back was sore and I took as it another sign that I should
take it easy.

Paul Raytheon entered and looked at me as if he'd just made a
discovery. "Well," he said, putting his hand over the mouthpiece of
his phone. "You'd like something to eat."

Paul Raytheon could look right into my stomach.

He had brought a cup of tea and there was a sandwich which
I looked at from a distance. I wondered what lay behind the fixed
glass case of Paul Raytheon's face but I did not know. Honesty,

perhaps — a love of peace and tolerance — the kind of well-being that is suspicious in the modern world.

"Do you think it's a coincidence that I met you?" he asked.

I held the cup of tea to my face, like it was stuck to my lip. "No."

I spoke into the tea and the word rippled. The tea was red, but black morsels of leaves turned. God knows what could be swimming in there.

"You're known around here," said Paul Raytheon. He pointed towards the upstairs. "You're known to the traffic wardens and they are known to me. Some of them have painted here before, in this very studio."

I shrugged.

"You're Guy Poynting," he said. "I recognised you straight away."

"Oh dear," I said.

Paul Raytheon was correct in his observation. Contrary to law, common sense and common practice, in a negligent manner that enhanced the probability of my inflicting injury on myself and other people, I was indeed Guy Poynting. Battery-operated, attitude incongruous, cable-joined Guy. Meta-analytic, consistent with the themes of his work — the loop-o-planes himself — Guy of Disguise — Poynting at the Wheel.

"Where the hell have you been?" asked Paul Raytheon.

Lies crossed my mind. More than lies. The well-known fable of the crow and the cheese — the suggestion to sing and the resultant loss of food. Innumerable analogues in which I am drawn, not into trickery, but into simple flattery of myself. I was off the ropes and general statements were my only defence.

"I've been about," I said.

"We're big fans of Liska's work," he said. "Really big fans. We've got respect for what she did."

There was the suggestion of perfect obedience behind the fine spectacles of Paul Raytheon, a clean creature perceiving accurately.

Man's filth and dislocation may have been revealed anew to Paul Raytheon, whose eyes witnessed everything like two washed pearls — but I was not at home to him.

"I'd really like to leave here," I said — but I knew that was going to be a problem. Paul Raytheon's disquisition had only just begun.

"Have a look at the studio first," said Paul Raytheon. "They're all big fans."

I doubted it, somehow. The more answers I heard, the more scared I became. Paul Raytheon cleared his throat like a tractor starting up, and the noise rattled terribly. It was just he and I together and he was considerably shorter than me. Me, irritatingly, still with no shoes.

"Excuse me," said Paul Raytheon. His head was like a drum with a smile painted on it. His neat shirt was tucked into neat trousers, and his Pentagon pager lay strapped like a legalistic application in his belt. Nothing was right about the man. "I'm on the phone," he said. "You go back to bed. Take it easy. It must have been tough."

"Are you artists here?" I asked him.

Paul Raytheon's admission came and he fidgeted with his pager while he talked.

"I'm a painter," he said. "But also we're activists for our art too. That's why I'm such a big fan of what Liska was doing. That was her vision, see?"

I climbed from the bed, still in those same amazing trousers.

"No need to get up," said Paul Raytheon. "Why don't you go back to sleep? They're still looking for you out there."

I looked into the much-tangled sheets — it was hardly a bath of bliss. The bed, in fact, was trouble, a catalyst for those bad dreams of Liska.

I went to bed as instructed. My hands were cold stripes of white where the blood thinned to an analytic trickle and I felt tired, like there'd been a drug in the tea. The day was over and Liska had left pale marks like contours in the approaching mud. She didn't say anything to me as I lay there — she just floated saucer-eyed before me, looking like she could have swallowed me whole — opened her jaw and pulled me to the sea bed. Liska waited, floating with the august solitude of the Minotaur, drifting the caves and corridors of her prison to snare those too blind to recognise a genius when they saw it.

I fell asleep and came back out again much later. The cupboard jutted out, a shadow, and the pile of suitcases on its roof formed their own shape as if they were about to jump. Police sirens rang far away, central to my silence, and as the day grew dark again, flickers in the corner indicated that Paul Raytheon was lighting candles.

I was hungry but still sulking. Hunger was categorised as one of my less pressing concerns and relegated to the back room of the brain. Paul Raytheon had left a sandwich on my bedside but I would not eat it. The sandwich sat with a couthy smile of cheese, minted into a square from which the spark of life had faded, and I recalled once more the genius of Duchamp.

There were certainly sublime moments in his art, but they were always contradicted by dissonances over which he had no control whatsoever. Duchamp could have spent weeks working on a sandwich like that.

43

☐   A knock on the door and the deep voice of Paul Raytheon welcomed a crowd of people to view me in bed. The guests entered with a respectful mumbling among themselves and stood around, nodding. Paul Raytheon came to the bedroom with a smile and more viewers arrived, conferring with each other while still smiling politely when they caught my eye.

"I'm getting up," I said, and I pulled myself from that sleepless bed, and walked unsteadily through the crowd.

Outside the Raytheon bedroom, the corridor was a mountain of books and print materials. There was a kitchen that doubled as a paint-mixing station, and in a studio at the end of the corridor there were several sculptures in various states of readiness. The area was lit with candles, which ultimately gave the place and people a religious feel that wasn't inappropriate. The crowd of young artists followed me from the bedroom and gathered behind me. I was stared upon as a totem — and nobody said anything — as if a joke were about to be played. Their knowledge of me was greater than mine of them.

"Are you all into the same art that Paul is?" I asked.

The question was passed from one to the other until they all nodded.

"Liska?" I asked — and the nodding continued.

I was going to ask the next question but Paul Raytheon spoke.

"We all feel the same about her pictures," he said.

An idea must have bonded this group and I felt again the patient acknowledgement of Liska's last wishes.

"Does that mean you all want to —?" But it was not a sentence I could finish.

I looked at my feet instead. My shoes were still missing and I owned no socks. Detailed examination of my toes reminded me that

I still had a desire to walk, and to keep walking.

"Not all of us want to destroy Liska's pictures," said a girl from the front of the crowd. "We still feel that her stuff being split up is against what she wanted, though."

"It's getting difficult," said Paul Raytheon. "There are only a few easy Liskas left to destroy, including the one in London. Mr Sharma misses Liska so much that it makes him sad to even look at her pictures."

"Me too," I said.

> cf. Charles Ray : *The Most Beautiful Woman in the World*
> (1993) Photo edition comprising a set of nine unique
> colour snapshots of the most beautiful woman in the
> artist's world.

"How do you know destruction is what Liska wanted?" I asked.

The girl next to me brushed the hair from her face and spoke — not to myself but to the group.

"Liska would have sacrificed her pictures herself," said the girl. "We all know what Liska wanted. We can't see any other way of dealing with people and actions that disturb her work now, and we believe we can keep her work in the state it was always intended to be. Unseen."

"Unseen?" I said.

I thought about it. Art as the most private realm of all — the imagination. Art in the world of dreams — that which makes the least of all social contributions.

"I don't know about unseen," I said.

Eyes large, nobody flinched. They were relaxed, their breath a calming drug for myself. At this pace, I thought, I might tranquilly become one of them.

"Unseen is the best way," said the girl. "You know what she wanted. You even had the idea yourself. You were in the art gallery when we destroyed those pictures. You wanted to destroy her pictures but we beat you to it."

Something concealed came to mind as if I'd known this argument before it had been put to me. "Are you from the gallery?" I asked, but I had already recognised her as the same girl who'd blasted those three Liskas with her homemade flamethrower, a fact that made me sense once more that I was in trouble.

cf. John Ramsay : *Let's Turn Glen Beagles Into Seattle* (2004) Hospital bed, plaster and enamel paint, blood pudding, artist [Glen Beagles], black marble hammers and firearms.

"This is Flo," said Paul Raytheon, and he put his hand on the girl's shoulder.

Flo smiled with such a variety of connotations that my heart stopped. She brushed hair away from her face to better see me. "You remember us don't you?" she asked.

Everyone was smiling apart from me. Mine was the odd face in the candlelight. Black tapped the kitchen window, beckoning me back to my bed, the only place where I had any authority in the world. But the show wasn't over for me yet.

"I remember your faces," I said, "but I don't know if what you did was correct."

The pair of them — the original art terrorists — they'd worn a disguise and plastic safety glasses that had been tailored to look like trendy frames — but now I saw them. The smiles didn't leave their faces when one of them said: "Guy, it was entirely correct."

"You're wanted by the police," I mumbled, to no effect.

The artists hovered before me, eight to ten faces, all with the same gooey look in the candlelight.

Now I have the picture, I thought. Dim night, stars positive, the subject's mood attenuated by the effort of running away from the police, and with over two thirds of the story done — the protagonist taking time to reflect upon the idiom in play — my life pro and dis — the unconvincing image of my attempted suicide tempered with another profusion of worries — until the hypothesis of self-murder is depicted once again in the deadness of the night. With my head buried in my shoulder the mundane was transcended and regret for leaving Liska was all I felt.

Later, the bedroom door was closed. The tiny streaks of candlelight that had glowed on the ceiling disappeared, and finally so did the sound of Mr Sharma's artists, who returned to their work or their pleasure, happy I expect, to have seen a living work like myself arrive among them.

44

■   Paul Raytheon was drinking coffee. He seemed more serious than ever, firm of face and bullish. His laptop was open and cables ran to ports and plastic junctions that should have been screwed into a wall. Beside the computer, and wrapped in tape, were several canisters of butane.

"Good morning," he said. It staggered belief that he could ever sleep, that his cheerfulness could ever be dampened by unconsciousness.

I stared at the rucksacks around his kitchen. Operation was imminent. A digital camera had arrived along with a printout ascribed NEGATIVE OUTCOME. Any art collector would know that Liska's work was a target, but according to Paul Raytheon's spreadsheet, there were still around 20 left from the 58 in her post-mortem stash. If these 20 were hidden or protected, this didn't bother him.

"I take it you have work to do?" I asked and Paul Raytheon nodded.

"We all have work to do," he said, "and I want you to come along."

I wondered if I had an option. I could sense that everyone knew what to do and that they had a part to play, and that was bound to extend to myself.

"You've got to help," said Paul Raytheon — and he didn't blink. I could barely look at him, he was so awake, so able to cope with the insanity of what he was suggesting. "You've got to come with us and help with the next few pictures."

"We'll get caught," I said. "They're going to be on the lookout."

"What are they going to do?" asked Paul Raytheon. His eyes instantly pressed a headache into my mind. "Are they going to arrest us all? Who cares? Even if they jail us then to hell with it. We're not hurting anybody."

"You wouldn't like it in jail," I said, and Paul Raytheon frowned. The steam from his coffee clouded out his spectacles.

"Damn it," he said, "we're not going to jail. These are the only paintings left and we're carrying out the will of a great artist. It can only end with us winning. Everyone will say so what? They'll see the genius of it. It's not as if we're breaking the law."

"You are breaking the law," I was going to say — but I am no expert in that area.

I longed for my shoes and a drink, but Paul Raytheon wanted to talk. Among the bones of my memories there had been a beautiful woman, and all that she'd said had been real. It's impossible to remember what someone has said after they've died.

"We're taking blowtorches again," said Paul Raytheon. "They're made from camping stoves. If you cut off the tube and put on this nozzle, it works quite well. The whole canister ejects in about fifteen seconds."

Paul Raytheon's laptop chirped to indicate that he had received some news. "Look," he said, and he waved his arm that I should join him.

Digitally reproduced on the screen was one of the sea pictures that Liska had painted in the summer we'd hiked up the coast and slept in a field. I'd not seen this picture for many months. The veins of colour in the water suggested the vessels of a heart and the painting offered the immediate sense that such a heart was beating all around us. The work was in London, I saw. Rather, you would have to say, what was left of it was in London — for some brilliant artists had attacked it — and two of them had been caught.

"There you are," said Paul Raytheon, and he read out the description of the event.

I could picture it — the sublimity of arrest, the bodily grace of being lowered into the cells — the battle made not against the banks or the government, but against art — the very heart of human care. In a photograph the artists responsible for the attack were led away by the police. Paul Raytheon enlarged the image with controlling mouse movements. In the picture, two scarecrowish English girls were seen. In the next image were the girls' chosen weapons, lighter fuel and matches, as well as kitchen knives. The work was just a burned painting now, a dead thing of beauty and it might as well have been removed from the galleries — although it was possible that the remains would stay where they were and become an attraction in their own right. Lunkenite society was more than capable of turning such destruction to profit, by charging admission for people to see the charred remains. They're just like that. Those art agents would make Narcissus pay to look at himself.

"So you don't mind being arrested," I said to Paul Raytheon, and he shook his head.

To be sure, Paul Raytheon looked too smart to get himself arrested. Even back in the gallery when he and Flo had been in disguise, they'd both seemed so organised that such a thing would be impossible.

"How many of you are there?" I asked but Paul Raytheon clicked on the computer and shook his head. "I don't know those guys but we're all pretty organised," he said. "They'd like to catch us but they'll never get us all."

"You'll never get all the paintings," I said. "All you're doing is making them more valuable."

"That's one less picture in London," said Raytheon. "Imagine if we do get them all. Wouldn't that be great?"

"Which one are we going for today?" I asked.

Paul Raytheon looked me squarely over. "Number 42," he said. "I just hope you don't get sentimental out there, that's all. We've got a job to do, and you're going to help us do it."

45

☐   We walked from the side door of the house into a gloriously cold and bright Aberdeen day. Up on Rubislaw Den, where Mr Sharma's massive house was, the stillness was as unreal as any of my dreams. At the side of the house, and amid the comic opulence of the bins, was an estate car that seemed huge next to the three of us. Paul Raytheon produced the keys and we all climbed in. The three of us drove away from Paul Raytheon's house towards Deeside.

The back seat of Paul Raytheon's car was filled with books. Paul Raytheon instructed that I do my best with them and I shovelled some on to the floor — but the books lay deep. Finally, I sat on top of the books and made myself comfortable, like a cat, shifting about until a nest had been made.

We drove along the North Deeside Road and past the Myrtle Gallery, and I stared out of the back window of the car, eyes open in a mad plea for light. When we cut back towards the town, we drove through a wide-open waste of grey-belt housing, and then we were free and in the country — enough to make me feel like I was leaving forever.

"Why do artists hurt?" asked Paul Raytheon. "All that pain, man. You can see it in so much of what they make."

"I don't know," I said.

Liska had felt a lot of pain in her life, but her pictures didn't show it.

"Crudely stated," said Flo, "a higher class of people than artists — generally and historically, their patrons — cling to all the money for aesthetic or political reasons. Respect is only feigned for human equality and respect for artists is non-existent. That's grounds for pain."

"Why did you become an artist, Guy?" asked Paul.

"I didn't become one," I said. "I was made that way, so that's why I never got a job."

"Either way," said Flo, "you become a slave of something. In the case of an artist, a system of patronage which means you still have to please the people with the purse-strings."

cf. Ken Currie : *Young Glasgow Communists* (1986)
Oil on canvas — the very last year, coincidentally, that Communism was ever mentioned.

I dug my feet around the back of the car, unsure of what to do about the books. Paul Raytheon had thrown his bags on top of this, making the books shift and slide.

"I picked them up from a house sale," he said. He shoved with his hand because some books had spilled into the front and were obstructing his use of the gears. "A house clearance," he said. "Somebody's entire collection. He died and his dog found him. Daschund. The Penguin Classics. Every single stomach-churning one of them. People build houses from this shit. They annex themselves to paperbacks as a surrogate spirituality."

"You go to a lot of house clearances?" I said.

"Yes I do," was the answer.

Despite all being paperbacks, there could have been nothing more uncomfortable for me to sit on than those books.

"These texts are a nightmare," I said trying to push a space in them.

"Artists feel the need to make a living," said Paul Raytheon, catching me in his rear view mirror. "It's not their fault that they're obliged to turn economic. You do what you can and if you can't sell your pictures you need another source of income."

"Have you sold any pictures?" I asked him and he stiffened.

"Way in the past," said Paul Raytheon. "I did sell pictures once. But not for a year now, and never again. I sell books and I enjoy it."

Flo agreed. "Our artwork is not for sale," she said. "It's not even to be seen. Sometimes we just conceive it, and don't even make it."

I was impressed. Liska's rules had been interpreted into the amusing rascality of not painting at all. Ironically, Liska's message appealed most of all to those who wanted to be artists but weren't sure if that involved them doing anything constructive. It was clear that in our era of hefty price tags, celebrity patronage and art being defined afresh each month, Liska had been on to something.

The car pulled off a roundabout and joined a row of vehicles forming a sociable line that led west towards a constantly changing horizon. I caught the side of Paul Raytheon's face, the trim beard, the expression conceited. The car banged over a dead pheasant on the road and I elbowed more books to the floor.

We drove further into Aberdeenshire and I prepared for the attack. I wondered how I would feel when I saw Liska's pictures.

Most likely, jealous, I thought.

How would I cope with a photograph of Liska's goldy-locks?

Liska moved from a breech in the rock and droplets floated in the black. Weeds sighed and the sand ran with crabs. I thought: Why didn't I jump with you when I had the chance?

46

■ Our target was Aboyne, a distant village of the fairest beauty. A line of trees napped along the roadside while the pink and lilac of the gardens shone with repellent brilliance. This was Aberdeenshire, where web developers worked in former farmhouses, and former farmers shopped in miniaturised supermarkets.

The car stopped under a rank of pine and Paul Raytheon examined a piece of paper. Pylons stood in sadness up a nearby hill and rain bled from the clouds, casting a nunnish grey on the village church.

"The duck restaurant," said Paul Raytheon, and he pointed along Aboyne High Street to the painted windows of an expensive eatery. Raytheon stared at the restaurant in true rapture. He gazed with the tranquil bearing of a saint.

"Deeside Ducks?" I asked.

I was curious to know where my love's paintings had wound up.

"That's the one," said Paul. "What a dumb place."

"What do I do?" I asked.

"Just play along with me," he said. "Our job is to distract the owner while the others do the business round the back."

Paul Raytheon worked his hands into the deep of his pockets and pulled out a tartan mobile phone. Flo was occupied with the satchel at her feet, saying uh, uh, to herself as she sang an imaginary song.

"Who are you calling?" I asked, and Paul Raytheon stopped typing and whispered, "We're not the only ones here."

Down the road, nothing. A circular village green, a sweet and gurgling stream and a weary weather vane. From round the corner arrived a woman with a pram. In the woman's hair were ribbons — her very perfection was as crisp as chimes.

Paul Raytheon sent his text message and asked Flo if she was ready.

"Sure thing," she said, and in the next second she had opened the car door and was gone. I watched Flo run up a grass lane that ran between Deeside Ducks and the next house.

"Great," said Paul Raytheon. "You and me now."

A handful of birds took off from a nearby tree and flew until they became little eyebrows in the sky. Paul Raytheon engaged me with an instruction: "Just play along with me."

I shrugged.

"When we get in there it'll be obvious. Stand clear if you see Flo or me with the blowtorches. It means we're about to burn the pictures."

"I get it," I said.

And I think I really did.

What I would do — I did not know — but I got the idea good and final. I remembered the gallery and I wondered if Liska would have torn down her pictures herself. I couldn't say.

Paul Raytheon's phone buzzed and words of instruction scrolled in a bed of liquid purple up its screen. The phone sat flat on his palm and once he'd finished he swept it into his pocket.

"Team two ready," he said.

Paul Raytheon wiped his brow and the woman with the pram glanced at us. I straightened my back and the pram creaked gently by. In the corner of my eye I saved the image of the mother, a pretty young woman in a skirt, drifting through a village that would be quiet were it not for Paul Raytheon's voice.

"Are we ready then, Mr. P?" asked Paul Raytheon.

"Don't call me that," I said.

More fragile, more broken, fuller of hope than ever, I stared at Paul Raytheon, feeling like I could crack up. Whatever Paul Raytheon had planned, I had little hope that we could get away with it and even less expectation that it would satisfy my desire to carry out Liska's aims.

Paul Raytheon opened the car door and pulled his bag to his

shoulder. The tools of his rebellion were blow-torches, knives and matches. The sight of Paul Raytheon in that village, planning his stage violence on Liska's work — I could see how art was never going to be properly handled in my lifetime.

"We're doing it!" said Paul Raytheon — and he was cheeky enough to give me the double thumbs-up.

As we passed the lane next to the duck restaurant, I saw no sign of Flo. Behind the duck restaurant were a quaint stable and a large red motorbike. We strolled to the front door of the restaurant where a CLOSED sign hung, as neatly mounted as any picture I'd ever seen, and Paul Raytheon pushed open the door and a bell pinged. I followed him in, creaking on the naked brown floorboards, counting the curious generality of ducks across the wall. The tables were set with white cloths and blood-red napkins. Duck motifs were here and there but most of the room was decorated with art that could have done with destruction in its own right. I was hypnotised by the silver sauce jugs and narrow oval plates, fascinated as to what may be about to happen. The cutlery was arranged for that night's feast with such wholesome sharpness that I began to feel scared myself. The man who appeared from the kitchen did little to allay this.

"We're closed," he said.

The man's irritation was clear. He wore a spotless apron and was higher than six feet — the bon viveur type who has eaten too much duck, I thought. Too much hog and fowl — it gives them that stupid / violent sheen. This man didn't need to be suspicious of us — the hatred was clear. Sagging unshaved skin — eyes like a deep-sea fish — a scrap of hair that had felt the tang of too much ointment.

"Gee," said Paul Raytheon. He pulled out a fictional voice from Ottawa, a dissembling tourist whine. "I heard this place would be open," he said. "I heard that it was great."

"No," said the duck guy.

The restaurant owner held a newspaper in one hand, a tiny coffee cup in the other. He looked like one of these pious men of the kitchen who like nothing less than to have their coffee interrupted. Just one of those pious men of the kitchen who was about to lose his paintings — I thought — like a man who's about to see his Liskas torched to hell.

"Gee," said Paul Raytheon again and turned on the spot, admiring the restaurant.

"I'll see you later then," said the duck guy, his face incapable of change.

Dead flesh attaches itself to the face of the eater, I thought. Just looking at the restaurateur, I knew he had all the virtue of a frog's turd. His lips were like poxied welts of meat and his hands an unhealthy smoker's grey. Skin the texture of honey-smoked ham.

"I'm very busy," he said. He was working through a rhetoric of expressions, each one employing greater hostility. I looked to Paul Raytheon for a lead but he was staring at the cruddy artwork on the walls.

"I've heard so much about this place," said Raytheon. It seemed obvious to me that he was killing time, or at least covering for something that was going on elsewhere. He may have been waiting for another cue but it seemed to me he was just dicking about for the sake of it. As these and other theories flowed loosely between the several species of hard cell between my ears, the attack on the restaurant began. It kicked off with what I thought was a gunshot from the rear of the building — a rocking boom that shook the building and shattered a glass.

We all looked at each other and it happened again.

A bang — the smash came quickly — and Paul Raytheon and I ran forward. The duck guy ran too. Paul Raytheon didn't get far, however, as his shoulder bag snagged on a chair — and I overtook both him and the owner and pushed the swing door to the kitchen. I hoped to hit the restaurant owner with the kitchen door but I missed and slipped, falling flat. Plain daylight turned black and a pain ran through my head. What I had slipped on, I didn't know

— grease or kitchen muck or blood — but what came next was the sound of feet running away, Paul Raytheon shouting "Stop!" and more shouting.

I realised I'd banged my head and so I relaxed and watched the ceiling. The day passed, cudgelled out in a timely procession of split seconds and my eyes found the kitchen clock.

All noise vanishes when you're on the seabed, in a way that you can't express anywhere else, and it was like that on the floor. Silence for earth people is merely the absence of noise — a definable moment that you find by accident — and in silence we forget the names for things, but I think it's really more likely that, in fact, things have no names to begin with. Maybe things are unidentified, like that time I spent watching the kitchen clock. Feet stamped by and it seemed that in the same moment, I was brought back to life by pain.

As I moved my head to rise there was another explosion. Rocking above me were pale stripped dead ducks, trailing from the roof by their necks. It was bad luck — a matter of fate — the element of chance. People will eat anything — it doesn't matter how base it is. They love the echoes of their own mortality.

> cf. Peter Ketter : *Uroboros (Yoga)* (1993) Fibreglass,
> wax, cotton. The figure of a man who appears to be
> chewing his own anus.

The kitchen rocked again. It wasn't a gunshot, but it was a definite blast from outside — perhaps a hammer hitting a steel wall. Whatever it was, that final bang shook the headache out of my ear and I started up.

The kitchen was a fairy-tale scene with its dead birds and racks of knives and boards. Some wicked cooking was afoot, all contrived from an old wives' tale. I jumped up and ran for the back door, and flew through to see what was happening.

Outside, the yard was messed with cooking litter, dustbins, loose feathers and an old roll of linoleum. In the centre of this, a man in a black mask held a plank like a paddle and as I arrived he used it to whack the duck guy's head. The duck guy recoiled, blood on his apron — and the tall man in the mask brought the plank down again and floored him. Flo was also there in a black mask and Paul Raytheon said from the back door of the restaurant: "Get the keys, man."

Paul Raytheon might have been speaking to me but I found the idea of the violence against this duck guy too surprising.

"Get the keys, man!" said Paul Raytheon again.

The man in the mask rifled the wounded duck guy, going through his pockets and jettisoning everything he found. He threw aside coins, cigarettes, receipts and a chain with a mobile phone on the end. It looked like Flo had been trying to blast her way into the converted stable and inside this stable I guessed were the pictures. Incredible, but the whole moment was terribly fulfilling. The stable doors were burned, and the owner was snaking towards them, not unlike the first wounded amphibian that crawled on a rock to see what it was going to be like to die on dry land, I imagine. The amusement brought out the sharpness of my knock on the head, and I giggled. Flo waited with her home-made flame-thrower and the masked man pulled at the wounded man's pocket, still hoping for a set of keys. For a moment, everything seemed light.

Several seconds passed in this daydream until the man in the black mask found a set of keys and set about the charred remains of the padlock. I looked down at the duck guy and wondered what next. His face was in his hands, from where he moaned and asked what was going on.

"Just shut up and face the ground," said Paul Raytheon, his voice trembling. It looked like there were going to be a lot of charges to answer here — although not for me. Paul Raytheon had now been party to a pretty ugly assault. When I next looked, the stable door was open and I ran in, looking for Liska's pictures.

Funnel-shaped vision, I call it — every image curving to the extended point of my world, where lay the target, two of Liska's paintings. Both paintings were of the sea, illustrated and perfectly measured, both awash with the tiny illustrations and messages that Liska worked into the waves. I remembered the paintings better than I'd expected — but that was all.

It wasn't that I disagreed with their destruction, but the paintings were so alive that I wanted to embrace them, so I ran forward with open arms. I pressed myself right into them and cuddled them both, breathing in their thick oily fumes in delight. I turned when I heard a scream.

The duck restaurateur had floored the masked man, and the masked man had been unmasked and was Joseph Gram. Paul Raytheon was yelling and the restaurateur was coming at me with a piece of wood. I held up my hand which he thrashed, leaving Flo to pull him down with some kickboxing to his legs.

With blood running from my hand, I crashed into Liska's paintings and as they collapsed I stuck my foot into a clay sculpture. Paul Raytheon was ready with his goggles so I tore the corner of Liska's painting and rolled away. Paul Raytheon's great moment had arrived — the high dignity of art was manifest — and the torch was applied with a lavish flame.

Boom and burn — that's how it went — and Liska would have loved it — a lavish and impressive flame!

Spend long enough with different people and you'll see that there's a correct way to do everything. A correct way to kill a duck, and a correct way to hide your feelings. There was a correct way to destroy art too and it was the Paul Raytheon method. I jumped back and was nearly burned. Paul Raytheon spread the flame to the left and right and waited until his canister had expelled. As soon as the flames dispersed, I grabbed at Liska's singed frames and tried to tear some more.

"Time to get out!" shouted Paul Raytheon.

Smoke filled the room and I noticed a store of more unplucked duckies on a rack. A fine insult to Liska, to stack her work with the dead, I thought. With that assurance I was bundled out of the stable and on to the grass.

Oh, they met in peace — Guy and the earth. It was comfortable down there, from whence the superior forms of men and women towered. I lay back, and as I gripped my sore hand, the restaurateur rose with his phone, presumably to call the authorities.

"Come on," said Paul Raytheon. "Get off the ground!"

"OK," I said, "I suppose I will."

But I didn't move. It was nice down there and it was certainly fine in that moment to be watching the others fight it out for the soul of postmodernism. I was as comfortable as I'd been in many a day.

47

☐   I was dragged from the duck restaurant face up in the grey of noon, as crows beamed from the trees. Joseph Gram bumped me from the stables and my arms scraped at the earth as I tried to take a handful of it with me. The earth came apart in my hands as Gram dragged me by the legs. I had managed to get a splint of canvas-stretcher and a fragment of Liska's painting into my pocket.

The greatest work of art is nothing, I thought, and can't compare to the artist who made it. Art's not worth money or love. It's not an inner discontent that makes people paint and sculpt but rather, the chance of salvation for the viewer. Art invokes love against the heretics — and the duck restaurant was a perfect example.

I think I was right. Art pricks the heart, but as you know by now, the resolute dictums of your talk destroys it — your looking at art, destroys art. The very aspect of the gallery — as Liska understood — is exactly that of a restaurant, or any other place of consumption. The point was a simple but devastating pinnacle of logic. As soon as a member of the public views a work of art, that work of art is in effect destroyed.

> cf. Martin Creed : *Work No. 227 The lights going on and off* (2000) The lights going on and off. Dimensions variable. 5 seconds on / 5 seconds off.

I was pulled from the scene while Flo filmed the incident for video posterity. That's right, I thought as Paul Raytheon helped to drag me along. All of this will be invaluable on YouTube.

The duck restaurateur was making for the back door of his restaurant. He was moving fast but Flo's camera was only interested in the erratic but thoroughgoing persecution of myself. I put my hands around my head.

"You fool," I heard as Paul Raytheon attempted to insult me in Ottawanese. "What do you think you were doing, man?" I glanced at the camera and its red light preached bitterly against my situation. I realised that this attack was, in itself, a strategic art-happening.

"Get up, goddamn it!" said Paul Raytheon. His bag slipped from his shoulder and a bunch of CDs spilled on the ground. He collected them and said, "Get up, goddamn it."

As I stared into the camera my mood changed. Distant faces would watch this in the future. I was being dragged through Aboyne while learned conversation took place on the other side of the screen, and I realised that it was time to get up. I was never destined to meet those paintings again and breaking them had left a void. Our goal had been achieved and the force of art-violence had won out, but I still felt like I was acting.

I picked myself up and followed the others to the car. Joseph Gram jumped on to the red motorbike, cursing me as he retreated. I held up my bleeding hand, an aspect of my star performance — and I moved on down the lane. Villagers stood at the corners of their gates and gardens, watching us without a sound. Paul Raytheon was cursing too. Blood ran from my hand and down my arm. I felt a weary sting in my head and wondered if they had got all the pictures.

I flung myself into the getaway car and lay on the books and said that I was sorry. I buried my head in the paperbacks while Paul Raytheon backed up the car, banged it off the pavement and then scraped it along something iron. Paul Raytheon pulled the car away and I heard the motorbike scream past. When we had made some sharp corners we were out of the village and running back to Aberdeen. This had been a brave thing to do, to destroy works of art — to outrage the art community. Give them nothing to appreciate, said Liska — and she pointed her bony hand. I was scared of Liska's hands because I was worried that she might offer me something from them. If I reached the hand and it pulled me into her soggy bank of weed, I feared that I would drown. Liska held up something — a remark or an obsession. She'd collected the remnants of her work since entering the sea, all the torn up and loathed pieces of seabed rubbish she could find.

I was out of breath and Paul Raytheon shouted as he drove the saloon car into the lordship of trees that led to Aberdeen.

"Jesus, what was that?" he screamed.

I gasped for breath. I was holding several scraps of the paintings in my hand. The scraps were like petals, faint as leafs. Flo was in the front seat and she turned to me with a frost-rent face and stared at me until I froze.

"What's going on?" shouted Paul Raytheon. "We had it planned. We were supposed to have it planned."

"That was a great thing you did," I said.

I suspected an explosion of tears from my tired eyes, because the brilliancy of mourning had hit me again. To remember hurts so much that the tendency is to forget — either that or a glow of fiction surrounds the past because memory has drifted and you've forgotten.

"That was truly special," I said, and put my head back in the books. "I'll get it right next time," I said and I closed my eyes.

I took a book in my mouth and chewed. The paper was sweet. I thought that in another life I might have been able to eat books and nothing else. The book was moist with tears, almost palatable to my coldness. I tried another book and cowered from the light. This book was older, browned leaves, a classic paperback flavour.

"That's right," said Liska. "You chew your book. Try that one too. It's new. The pages have more of a chemical taste. It's not poisonous but if you chew it fast enough you'll get high."

I dug my face in. Back covers and open pages, ruts and broken spines, sun-frazzled books pegged against each other in piles on the floor and over the seat. Out of the window, passing treetops rid the world of pain, and thoughts of blame dissolved. I was broken-hearted when I thought of Liska now, but I knew I wasn't about to give up on her final works.

"I'll do better next time," I said, but Paul Raytheon shook his head.

"No next time for you," he said.

48

Paul Raytheon slowed the car and I sat up. In the corner of the Forestry Commission car park at Counteswells, Joseph Gram was leaning on his motorbike. Under the firs he was like an enormous executioner awaiting the guilty party.

Paul Raytheon opened the car door and myself and several books fell out. Joseph Gram steadied his motorbike and frowned.

"Look at you," he said, "you haven't changed. Where have you been?"

"I'm sorry," I said. "I couldn't help myself when I saw the pictures."

"My bad," said Paul Raytheon. "Mr Sharma said we shouldn't take him."

Joseph Gram leant towards me, ever clever, and deeming himself in charge. He gripped my shoulder and I looked into the low side of his face.

"It must be hard without her," he said.

Joseph Gram examined my hand and I looked away, seeming to find Liska's face in the fir trees. Liska didn't look nice in daylight — she had no eyes and her body was a rack of vodka-stained bones. Liska's face rose from the horizon, which at this point was the bated grey of the forest. A small fish swam out of her eye socket.

"He's been eating books," said Paul Raytheon.

Joseph Gram let go of my hand.

"I was looking forward to meeting you again," said Joseph Gram, "but you seem to have caused a little trouble."

"We can't take him out again," said Paul Raytheon — and Flo nodded. Joseph Gram looked at me as if I were a painting myself. I mean that he cocked his head in appreciation, like the well-mannered individual of today, the suggestion of an inquisitive pose.

"I don't know," said Joseph Gram. "He could be valuable to us yet."

"Yeah?"

"I think so."

Gram showed Paul Raytheon my wretched hand. "This is blood — and it's just the start," he said.

"Don't be so portentous!" said Paul Raytheon, and he combed his hair with his sleeve, settling his mind.

My palm nipped and I still felt a trickle of blood. The others were talking about Liska and I was counting the striations on my trousers. The destruction of art might have been a new beginning for Paul Raytheon and Joseph Gram, but it was the end of the line for me. They're just getting out of painting by doing this, I thought. They can't even be bothered to splash a little paint about.

> cf. Franz Kline : *Untitled Insane Amount of Abstract Expressions* (c.1955) brush and ink on paper, signed KLINE lower right.

I didn't want any more art-anarchists, leftists, exemptists, irritationists, dopists, controversialists, or symbolic systemists with recited doctrines. I paused, concentrating on the natural activities of the forest, and thought about handing myself in. Perhaps I had hated art all along and, as with so many other people, my reaction had been to create more of it. All my life I had been an artist. I had let the idea run riot fifty seven minutes every hour. That left two minutes for dreaming — thirty seconds for doubting — fifteen seconds for loving the world — seven seconds for resolving that I could do something about it, and four seconds for high consciousness. For two seconds of each hour I stared at my hands or felt my trousers — and for one second every hour I allowed my normally sublimated sexual desire a chance to think what it wanted. Half a second every hour of the day was spent in fright, and a half of that was spent in remembering my childhood. You can calculate my free time from there.

Joseph Gram talked about Liska with Paul Raytheon. Gram looked his usual gracious self, ritually dressed in black, with his customary up-to-the-minute watch.

"Hey, Guy," he said, and I turned from my day-dreaming. Joseph Gram, my number one fan, was calling me.

"We're going back to the studio," he said. "A few people to see."

Who was I to disagree? I did what my protectors said, so long as I was living. Once I was safely dead again, then I shouldn't have to worry. Was anybody brought back to life as often as I was?

49

☐   Art hates me now and believes me to have cheated it out of a free ride. But look at postmodern people, those dabblers in public print, speakers of journalese, the many copy chiefs and know-it-alls whose lexicon is the television documentary.

An awful assumption was made about art when Liska and I were alive, insofar as when people saw a work of art, they expected edification. At the same time, the ultimate introduction to our society was that the arts were blamed for the violent ills which plagued it. Nobody believed a criminal back then when they said *God or the Bible made me commit that crime*, but people were still content to pin violent acts on Marshall Mathers (for example) and his wicked films and video games. For edification we had artists shitting into cups — artists who dissected their own families for public kicks — those who liked to shock and those who like to joke. Back then, we were edified most of all by the terrifying emptiness of the CONCEPT. Art was proclaimed through a tight sphincter of media excitement and the rave viewing public treated itself to expressions of violence on violence, and they still found art respectable, no matter how vile or drab its perpetrator. So long as the artist was making a statement, the public could understand and assimilate the work. The attitude of instructed people as regards art had changed, and it was never changing back.

Heery said that new words for art worked much better in Gaelic — and he was right.

cf. *abartach*   talkative
     acartha   profit
     achdartha   methodical
     adhart   pillow

aghart	progress
aimbeart	distress
àineart aich	yawning
ainneart	force
ballart	boasting
cartaighim	Irish — cleaning out
eadartha	noon / milking time
gartiugud	whiling the time away
martadh	maiming
neart	strength
oirbheart	good deed
pailleart	a box on the ear
rabhart	senseless talk
sagart	priest
tochartagh	Irish — winding yarn
tairbheartach	profitable
vainneart	wallowing

This was a theological point, given the spiritual importance people placed on their art. Any technique concerned with revealing more about the relationship between ego and commerce could not be bad, and so I think Heery was on to something there.

The final lesson was that all of this art and business leads us only into trouble — equally and together. There is only one cathedral and it's made of flesh — so fill it up with duck meat and read on.

■ "I've got a bad feeling here," said Paul Raytheon as we drove into suburban Aberdeen. "I don't know if we can get away with this anymore."

There were more pictures of Liska's to destroy, but Paul's confidence was falling apart as if all the staples had been taken out.

"We gotta lay low," said Raytheon — and I sniggered with attitude.

I banged on the car roof and shouted: "How many left?"

Paul Raytheon didn't answer, but Flo had a notebook which contained her latest calculations on the subject and she estimated there were in the region of 14 remaining pictures. There were the so-called zero-rated lots for sale on the internet and another three dozen that had vanished at a seller's premium from Mr Sharma's post-quietus garage sale — and there were a handful that had disappeared altogether.

I know I can do it! I suddenly thought. Destruction of beauty in one sense, but robbing society of its ill-got treasures on the other.

"We've got to finish this off," I said. "We've got to get them all!"

"You got in the way," said Paul Raytheon, and he ignored me after that. He had determined that I was counterproductive to his group's assault on the pedantic public consumption of my best friend, art.

Liska didn't say anything either. She'd always leave me to my own decision-making. Was it a good idea to destroy Liska's pictures or was there a better way to save the world? These collectors and sponsors were the same people who'd either directly or indirectly, given a lot of artists a lot of money — but Liska offered no opinion. She just sat there like a lump of coral, her hair floating like weed. I knew what I wanted though, and I was sure that I would be able to do it the next time.

☐   Paul Raytheon steered his estate car into the time-defying grandeur of Rubislaw Den. We drove along a five-hundred-yard row of mansions to where a line of even larger houses discharged their wealth into the earth. We slowed to a sedate pace that was intended to fit the mood of the neighbourhood, and pretty soon we pulled up next to Joseph Gram's motorbike, outside Mr Sharma's miracle mansion. Lightless windows, crosshatched with black glass, looked on a bulb bed where saplings had rooted shoots. The sun lined up its evening rays behind the chimney, while unforeseen forces of fate coated the eaves and points. A dog came sniffing round the birches as the evening burned out shadows in the driveway, and Paul Raytheon stuffed a sports bag between the two front seats and scowled at me.

"Fill it with books," he said.

Pondering the books, the flaps and leaves, the covers marked with crits and pics, I could only make the one conclusion — another suicide. They'd tie the bag of books to my leg and drop me in the harbour. Once the books are water-logged, I thought, the literature will continue its onward course to the rust and silt beneath the waters.

I filled the bag with paperbacks like I had been asked, and Flo joined me. She scooped away while Paul Raytheon pouted his lips and waited.

I finished up and looked at the Sharma mansion for signs of life but there was nothing doing. It was like a brothel — net curtains concealing the secret economy of the interior.

"Take the bags inside," was Paul Raytheon's command as he slipped the car door closed.

I followed him, my rational pneuma draining fast, and when he reached the front door of the house, Paul Raytheon rang the bell, which chimed inside with the mellow bobbing of tubular gongs. The bell faded with the last of the sun in leaf patterns on the houses opposite. The chime grew faint below the heavily scented blossoms of the evening, and I noticed the name of SHARMA on a brass plate.

"Front door, this time," said Paul Raytheon to me, as he stood to attention, calm as a good churchman.

A second later, Mr Sharma opened the door and gazed upon me. It was the same old tanned Mr Sharma. He wore his universal brown suit, and in the top pocket of his jacket were the folded spectacles with which he spied on all our faults.

"Come in," said Mr Sharma, speaking to us all.

So generous a proposal could receive but one response, and we walked forward in a line.

At home, I noticed that Mr Sharma wore sandals, and not the super-Guccis of yore. He bore the same nobility he had used to get his thievish hooks into Liska's work, but his confidence had increased. I was not comforted and as Flo put down her bag of books, I dropped mine also. Paul Raytheon hung the car keys on a handy peg and helped to guide me in.

"I can't believe you're still with us," said Mr Sharma — this comment for me.

In the gritless dark of the hall, Mr Sharma's hair was like a dunghill, attached to his head through magic. There were two swords crossed on the wall and I gazed at a little model of a man riding on an elephant. Looking at the little man I had the idea that Liska must have known that I couldn't jump off that ferry.

"Could you take your shoes off please?" asked Sharma, and I grasped at my footwear and pulled.

Was I supposed to have jumped?

Liska really did jump — but what happened to her next?

Sharma held open a curtain to the living room, and I once more relinquished my shoes to Paul Raytheon. There wasn't actually a figure on the elephant, I noticed. It had only been the shadow of a plant, falling on the base of an incense burner.

Behind the curtain was an open conservatory where computer terminals crowded on several tables. At the television, gallantly decked out in High Street gear, were the contented youth of Babylon, and with them was Joseph Gram, lying by a woman on a sofa while another woman stretched on a rug, with one hand in a pizza box.

"You could at least have hidden your bike," said Paul Raytheon as we approached.

Smoke curled from the settee where Joseph Gram and the woman stretched. Joseph Gram was already dressed for home, in sandals, and next to him a pot of flowers acted as an ashtray.

"I'll do it later," he said. "These girls are working very hard."

"I can see that," said Paul Raytheon, his voice more moral than ever.

I stood spare while Joseph Gram put out what he was smoking, lowering it to the plant pot carefully so that he didn't have to turn his attention from the screen.

The woman on the sofa bent her head backwards.

"Could you fetch me a glass of wine?" she asked.

The bottle was near so I took the opportunity to serve us both, myself by the neck. If Liska is here, I thought — in the house or in the garden — in the form of art or seaweed — in person or in memory — then I will need a drink. Chilled wine poured into my body and once I had had my fill, I handed the bottle over.

"We've got a room for you downstairs," said Sharma. "It would be great to put some of your skills to use."

I knew exactly what Mr Sharma meant. Mr Sharma knew that I wasn't going to stick around any longer than I had to.

"Do you want me to help with the rest of Liska's work?" I asked bravely, but he shook his head.

I could see Liska despairing. The sigh that oozed out of her filled the sea, it washed over the room, and behind it was her face, telling me to get out of there — telling me that I had gone too far — that I should never have left that ferry boat alive.

cf. Jenny Holzer : *Die Fast and Quiet...* (1987) Red writing on aluminium. 'Die fast and quiet when they interrogate you or live so long that they are ashamed to hurt you anymore.'

A mobile phone rang from within the sofa and Joseph Gram felt inside. He paused the film and stuck the mobile to his ear. "Ya!" he shouted, in a new voice entirely.

I glanced out of the window, into the thawing mist beneath the trees. Paul Raytheon was leaning on the back of a chair. His was the look the farmer gives the sheep at the very last moment.

"Guy's got to rest," said Sharma. "We didn't want anyone to get hurt. Paul, I don't think we should go for any more paintings in this fashion. Guy, I want you to stay here tonight and you're not to leave the house until I say so."

Joseph Gram said shoosh and stuck out his hand. The woman next to him cast a long bolt of smoke and ended her cigarette in the plant-pot.

"That's what you should do," said Gram on the phone. "I mean — there are two sorts of players in this game, and one set are always going to be ahead of the other."

The caller spoke and Gram listened, and we waited to see the outcome. Gram didn't lose a second's composure. His was the most gentlemanly, unbuttoned ease.

"You'll meet people like that," he said. "Everyone wants you to take their advice but only you know the real value of your work. Take it from me."

Sharma stood like a block of sandstone, his arms folded and his beige suit perfect.

"The quickest way with an artist like you," said Gram, "is to float you like you were a company. It would be like offering shares in you — if you know what I mean. You know — intellectual property. You like the idea of creating money — but you're an artist. So we'll ensure that we've sold your next ten paintings before they're even painted. We'll float you and you'll love it."

Paul Raytheon nudged me and Sharma said, "Come on," and he led us back towards the curtain. I heard the film begin again as we walked into the hall.

I followed Mr Sharma to the basement. Above, there were tiers of stairs to nowhere, with faint music at the summit. There was a third floor, and I knew the house to have another wing also — but I was going down, not into the light but into the protective captivity of the cells.

Liska put her hand up from the trench. Her eyes were two brown spots and her hair had gathered in a nest of snarls. I was on my way to the basement of Mr Sharma's decadent art base but I couldn't wait to get out again and break more art. I appreciated Liska's vision more than ever — or at least I thought I did — I'm sure I wasn't imagining it. Liska was somewhere in the sea, floating on the prolonged sighs and groans of the current — and I lived in the outer firmament, now on a mission to end what she'd begun.

52

■   A provoking episode indeed. I had been immersed in the destruction of art (and art's destruction of art!) for so long, that by this time I was so rubbed raw in my sensibility that something as soft as a tube of paint might have broken me. I was dead to the idea of making paintings for a living — either that, or I had stumbled upon an artistic way out.

Mr Sharma and Paul Raytheon led me to the basement — the laundry room to be exact — and I was positioned in the doorway. It was even possible that I was about to be erased.

"So little of the artwork we make here is ever exhibited," said Paul Raytheon, "Once the artists' work has reached a certain stage we sell it. The artists become their own property and product."

"I'm not impressed," I said. "Artists might need money, but you're not going to solve that by giving it to them."

"Chin up, Guy," said Mr Sharma. "We're all going to finish Liska's work — just not together. In the meantime, please be kind enough to stay in here and let us do it without your input."

He was offering me the laundry room, accommodation with two tumble dryers and a whole lot of underwear.

"Part of what happens to you," he said, "will be decided by yourself. You are wanted by the police, like Paul and Flo. But you will not be caught. Think for a few hours, and if you want to, after that, I can give you a room upstairs. You'll have everything you need."

"Not privileged to the Utopian food trolleys of the upper floor?" I asked — and Sharma shook his head and in appeasement pointed to a box of crisps in the corner. A multibox of crap crisps — the biscuits of the dim-witted.

"They'll keep you going," he said.

"Crisps?" I asked — and Sharma nodded.

"You can have as many as you like," he said.

"Where are Liska's paintings?" I suddenly asked him.

I cast an eye to my escape route but it was blocked by Paul Raytheon. Mr Sharma looked at me long. His eyes reminded me of a bug's eyes, dry balls staring and nothing there.

"You can't see her paintings," he said.

I would have protested but I sensed danger. In the doorway, Paul Raytheon's head balanced on his mauve and loose-knit sweater.

"What are you going to do with them?" I asked.

I thought that Mr Sharma was about to say "I'm going to sell them," but he stopped and thought for a moment.

"Art should always be ahead of everything else," he said. "Liska left a body of work that is now impossible to display, but her ideas have been inspirational. When all of Liska's pictures have been destroyed, not only will the ones that I own achieve the value she deserves, but she will have started her own art movement. Great joys came into Liska's life but also great sorrows. She may not have known it but Liska summed up the question of art and its relationship to business. That's why none of the artists here exhibit. Last night I went to a party where people were bidding for a work that didn't exist. The work only existed because I told them it existed. It was just an idea that someone had, but we've been building its importance for some time. I grieve the loss of Liska but she knew what she was doing. Hers is a valuable experience. All of the artists here have their values. The artists refrain from showing their work but only on the promise of more support. People see it as priestly — and the artists live the life they enjoy, working without scrutiny. Paul sells paintings and his conceptual pieces all over, but I don't think he's ever held a brush. Paul Raytheon is the artist of the future — in fact — I don't think Paul will ever produce anything again. Not one single piece."

"I want to see the pictures you've got left," I said, but Sharma shook his head.

"I invested in them and they are mine," he said.

Sharma closed the laundry room door and locked it. Sheets and towels hung in rows, and shirts lay on accurate racks. High slits on the wall allowed the last light of the day to shine, while in the corner was a fat brown leather sofa, like the back end of a beetle.

Mr Sharma's blobby head appeared at the frosted window in the door.

"Just until the heat is off," he said to me, and footsteps walked away and I wondered where I was, what I was doing, what I did for a living and how I might ever enter the infinite paradise of my soul.

> cf. Mel Ramsden : *Secret Painting* (1968) Two parts : Letraset on cardboard reading : The content of this painting is invisible; the character and dimensions of the content are to be kept permanently secret, known only to the artist. Acrylic on canvas, black.

Great joys came into Liska's life but also great sorrows. How could Sharma know anything of the sort?

I tried to work out if there was a hope of escape, but it didn't seem too promising. I was underground in West End Aberdeen and all my deadly foes were waiting for me in the house above.

"Let me out!" I cried — but nobody responded.

I sat on the naked plank of an old bench, irate and harried. There was no rope to hang myself but plenty sheets. Under the sheets was a large-scale trouser press, which offered me the most painful suicide there had ever been. Those who commit suicide in trouser presses are particularly masochistic. And there were crisps. I could be the first man to crisp himself to death. If you eat enough acidity regulator you curl and crimp yourself into spasms which can be fatal. If the Acidity Regulator fails, you may suffocate yourself with the empty packets.

"Let me out!" I cried — but I shouted in vain.

The destruction of Liska's paintings occurred to me again, and I banged my hands on the door. I wanted out of Mr Sharma's house and I needed to be with Liska.

"What makes you think that?" said a voice — a voice from within the sheets.

Somewhere in the room there was a good piece of advice. Blackness has a texture, which is why Liska could often unknot herself from the darkest corners of the world and speak to me. Now I believed that she was going to appear in the sheets. Mr Sharma had destroyed art in order to raise prices — and I wondered at the contradiction. The only way for me to achieve my end was at Mr Sharma's expense — and so I had to destroy his collection. Liska was dead and there was no way they could help her now — and even if they thought they could fool me, I would still escape and destroy what of Liska Mr Sharma had tucked away.

53

☐   I may have succeeded as King of the Laundry Room. Someone has to fill these roles. The problem was that I didn't stay long enough to try my hand.

The door was solid. The window was narrow. The sheets were damp. The crisps were rank. I couldn't fit down the drain. I thought of tumble-drying myself to death — but no. There were no sounds from upstairs and I had the crazy impression that I was not wanted. I filled one of the washing machines with soap and switched it on, and for twenty minutes watched the foam until it started to leak out of the sides.

I poured a bag of crisps into my mouth but they had no flavour, something that caused my anger to resurface. If, like Samson, I could have torn that building down, I would certainly have done so. The survivors would only find soap bubbles and crumbs. My end was all I had. Footsteps stirred in the corridor and a familiar, affable breath whispered outside the door. I knew who it was.

"Is that you, Paul?"

Paul Raytheon stood on guard outside the door. He was still annoyed with me for what I'd done at the duck restaurant.

"If you hadn't tried to protect the paintings, nobody would have been hurt," said Paul Raytheon through the door.

I heard the anorak rustle and I stuck my hand in more crisps.

"I need the car," I said to Paul Raytheon. "I want to get out of here."

"You'll get out of here," said Paul Raytheon — and he coughed.

"I really need the car," I said. "I know where there are more pictures. All of Liska's pictures. Notebooks and other drawings."

Paul Raytheon snorted. His rustle came closer to the door and he said, "You're lying," and after that, he departed, tutting.

When Paul Raytheon was gone, I put the washing machine on to a spin cycle and stood teeteringly on top of its shaking white box and looked along the old shelves. Perhaps I could build a bomb, I thought. Some marine soap and a wash ball, soaked in sodium carbonate and beaten with a bath brush, then wrapped in a serviette. That would make a puky splash on their coats — and I could run for it.

In the end, however, I was saved by underwear.

Aren't we all at times?

That's right — it happened by chance — pants. It was Adam's crutch. I was saved by a pair of clean green sexies — the small clothes of freedom.

It was about an hour after Paul Raytheon had left when somebody once more tried the handle of the laundry and unlocked it. With the door wide open, a woman in towels entered, a young woman like the other ones — and she smiled as if she didn't mind my being there. She wore two towels. Yes, one for her head and another for her body, and she carried a phone and a glass of wine and set them down while she looked around the room.

"You're locked in," she said — and she looked through a basket and found the clothes she needed.

"Mr Sharma locked me in," I said.

The washing machine entered a higher dimension of noise.

"Oh, him," was all the towel girl said.

I excused myself and left, down the corridor towards the stairs. At the top of the stairs I met Joseph Gram winding up another conversation on his phone, a little less technical this time. Joseph Gram closed his phone and began with me.

"Are you staying?" he asked, clipping his phone to his dressing gown.

"Not for long," I said.

I looked up the tall well to the top floor of the house. Joseph Gram passed me by, smiled like an exhibit in a ghost train, and followed the towel girl through the curtain and into their living space.

Once the curtain had closed, a relative silence mixed with the luxury. In this trenchant moment of excitement, all I could make out was the faint sound of a television and the slowing of the washing machine below me.

I walked to the first floor, a crescent balcony with a line of open doors, behind which were bedrooms and untidy sitting rooms cluttered with plates, books and clothes. There were six such rooms on the first floor, in one was a man reading a woman's magazine. In another room was a rowing machine and on it was a man in exercise clothing, tight strips that made a separate country of each buttock.

In the last room, some laptop users looked over papers and watched a business broadcast. The television muttered pleasantly and the laptop users pushed themselves far into their beanbags. One woman spoke on a phone — she was stretched out with her legs pointing from a pleated skirt. She spoke gently while the rod of her pen doodled numbers on a pad. The laptop users clicked in their red and white pit. Red on the walls and red in the furnishings, white in the expressionist art that hung there. Red in the wine-coloured carpet and white in the cushions on which they sat. White in their faces and in their ashtrays and plates. White in their paper notes and red in their lips.

A door opened behind me and out came an artist. I knew she was an artist because she had a paintbrush. Her sweater was dug with clay and her eyes were as bright as brass.

"Hello," she said, cigarette in mouth, amused by something.

I looked inside this artist's room to see what she'd been doing.

This was evening, and everything was dying, save for the patch of light where the woman had been working, a bright shape around a desk. I stepped in and saw the wares — rack over rack of paintings, work sold but never seen. There with it, was the most valuable work of all — that of Liska.

I entered the room and looked at Liska's pictures, one at a time. Mr Sharma had done well. He had at least four of Liska's pictures, all sea abstracts, textured with her trademark twist. He also had the largest of the 58 in that room, which was an image that for me at least, disclosed Liska's daytime love affairs — cups, bottles and birds — thin bodies and dry flowers.

One at a time, I withdrew the paintings, my eyes a mist in the face of Liska's heroic constancy. I thought about these pictures' value and the cynicism of holding on to them while destroying others on the side.

Let's face it, I thought. A bold effort, but art and its buyers should stay the way that Liska loved them — as friends, not collaborators. When it comes to the point where truth is sacrificed then art can only be its honest self, even if that self is childish and rebellious. Art is like a child and therefore should never be lied to. There's nothing worse than being told you're loved, for example, when all you are to some people is a prize.

At the bottom of the sea Liska was free of the solid appendages of both art and money. Liska unstopped her eyes and water flowed into the empty sockets with no resistance. Flowering creepers of seaweed perfumed the water. Liska lay out of reach of the trawling nets and the debris cast from the North Sea tugs — although she sometimes looked up and watched the occasional fisherman die of resistance to what she'd found so peaceful. Much of Liska's ocean bed was prefigured in her pictures, perhaps in the lack of connection a viewer could make with the darkness. Liska had worked out her own darkness, and now without burden, she was free to enjoy it.

I didn't need Parry's old pen or Paul Raytheon's blowtorch — I used the artists' tools nearby. I worked quietly at first but made more noise as I speeded up, and the more I tore, the more I wanted it to be over. There would be a point when I would be too blind to see what I was doing and I'd start tearing up other people's work too. The sculptor in the sweater returned and screamed and ran for help. I was now tearing Liska's pictures with the most frantic slashing actions and I burst through one frame and then another. I knew that I had to be comprehensive if I were to beat Mr Sharma at his own game. Remember, I thought. These people can sell anything — so I must make this into as little as possible.

By the time the laptop users had been drawn towards the damage, I was making short work of the remains. Destroying half a dozen paintings takes it out of you. There's the wooden frame and then the canvas itself and although I tried to smash bottles across the stretchers, not all of them would break. My arms were tired, because painted canvas is tough, and I knew then that you can't destroy it enough. You've got to destroy it several times over.

> cf. Gary Hume : *Four Subtle Doors* (1989/90) Gloss painted on canvas — executed in about 4 minutes flat.

That's the trouble with canvas — you've got to pull it in the right place, because the fibre tears so neatly. Most of the time when you destroy paintings, you're left with a remnant that looks quite pleasing in itself — and that's why I started stuffing the remnants into my pockets, and that's when they came for me.

When the first laptop user grabbed me I howled and thumped him. I shouted that they were all mad and I tried to break past them. It didn't hurt when they stopped me — not in comparison to what else was happening. They had all played rugby for so long that I didn't have a chance. Still — I wriggled out of the scrum and crawled my way to freedom, still managing to hold many scraps of what had been Liska's work.

In the corridor and on the stairs more laptop users had appeared, most of them in innocent states of undress. Joseph Gram was there and he too had lost most of his clothes.

"Guy, no," he said — the minimum of protest.

"I've given up arguing!" I shouted. "You people always win!"

A wistful Joseph Gram watched me in pity as I darted for the stairs. He made signals to the other laptop users that they were to head me off.

"Grow up now," he said — and I dribbled to show that I would not grow up. Once I'd dribbled enough to make Joseph Gram back off, I headed again for the banister in the hope that I could slide to freedom.

The last thing I remember?

The final realisation of my own wretchedness and an uncertain gesture that made me hold my hands up as if I had seen a gun. Artists on one side and laptop-users and towel people below. I was flanked and outclassed — out-bred and outdone. They moved towards me and I backed down the stairs. The laptop users held cigarettes and the artists held brushes. The towel people tapped their wine glasses together and the artists quivered to anticipate the next surprise. One must choose, I thought, and there are so many cosmic forces on offer. Whether through light or darkness, the primeval urge to create chaos out of the order was still strong, and I vaulted the bannister in an attempt to land like a cat on the ground floor.

54

▓ "What are we going to do with you?" asked Mr Sharma. Behind him, his staff looked down on me. They were all bloody smiling. I lay on my back and I could see why the beautiful people idolised Mr Sharma. They knew they had to serve somebody, and he had offered to be that entity.

"You won't work with my staff," said Mr Sharma, "and despite your talent, you're no use as an artist. I think I'll have to throw you back in the sea — like they do with the little fishes that are too young to sell."

I didn't argue because I was concerned that I may have been paralysed. Also, I should have to say that I agreed. The sea was the best place for me, fishing metaphor or not. The sea was, in fact, the only place for me and I fantasised for a split second about being with Liska, unseen, and nibbled on the edges by the copapods, and the other degenerate bottom dwellers.

"I don't know what to do with you," said Mr Sharma. "Have you broken your back?"

I shook my head. Mr Sharma was a man of stone, tense, with the bearing of a Greek statue, making sure that wherever he was, he was still the focus — it gave him that divine edge.

"You just don't get it, do you?" he said.

This from the cool millionaire creator of heaven and earth, and all that crept about on it.

"Just help me up," I said. "Get me to the door and I'll take it from there."

Ceremoniously, they picked me up from the floor and walked me to the front door of the mansion. I felt like I had lived all of life. I wasn't sorry to be leaving, my only issue was that now, even among the artists, I was an outsider once again. I said goodbye to them, but most of them had lost interest in me, and by the time I was on the threshold they had all but drifted away. It was early in the evening and my pockets were empty, a fact which gave me one more idea.

"Can I borrow some money?" I asked.

The sense of disappointment in Mr Sharma's face was evident, but I butched it out, staring him down, my open palm held out.

"This is goodbye," said Mr Sharma sternly, and he strolled back inside, in search of his wallet. While I was alone for that second, I unhooked the car keys from where Paul Raytheon had hung them up. Another perfect crime.

When Sharma returned I took his money and said thank you.

"Tell me," said Sharma, "you'd both planned to kill yourselves hadn't you?"

"Yuh," I said, making eye contact with the figure on the twenty pound note he'd given me.

"Why would you want to do that?" he asked.

I wanted to tell Mr Sharma the truth. It seemed that for myself and for Liska there was a minimum of difference between being here and not being here. You could have said that we both had depression, but that was a classification that wasn't useful to us as we'd both exhausted it long ago, certainly before we'd met. It wasn't about art either, because art had just been a way to deal with life. We'd just met and found that we shared a common interest.

"We wanted to be together," I said to Mr Sharma — and I trudged across the gravel, feeling his curious eyes drilling into my back. At the gate I stopped and turned but he had already closed the door, which was fine, because it allowed me to return to the green Mercedes. I stepped into the car and was pleased to find several bottles of Baal's beer awaiting me in the passenger seat — a fitting accompaniment to my finale.

55

☐   As I was gulping — with what strenuously affected Stoicism, fit to alert a street of degenerates to my dietary virtue — I'm sure you can picture for yourself — as I was gulping then, at my own bottle of Baal's Beer, the only food or drink to be found in Mr Sharma's green Mercedes, I was awakened to the weighted significance of the fact that I had business to attend to, but as was often the case with me, I wanted to play first. For a moment I sat in the driver's seat of Mr Sharma's car, enjoying my beer, happy that I was leaving the accursed studio where art and business rode the same pony.

I started the engine of Mr Sharma's car and its sound, so sweet and certain, decided me upon my mission. As I pulled away, Mr Sharma appeared at the front door of his house, and with an amusing mix of disobeyed authority and damaged pride, yelled something like: "*Oi! You Little Bastard!*"

Too late for me, however. I was bound for Anna Lunken's house, not to collect but to destroy — not to view but to pillage. Not to put too fine a point on it, to destroy as many pictures as I could before my time was up. Not to be too mean about it — to kill off Mr Sharma's last investment.

As swiftly as a bird, and as subtly as internal combustion could arrange, I darted from Mr Sharma's gravel driveway and on to Rubislaw Den. I pointed the car up the hill and pressed the pedal, and away I went, my first target being the screaming carriageway of the Aberdeen city bypass.

I relaxed in Mercedes leather and opened another beer while the solid nothingness of road travel took over and I entered a dream. Lights flashed in a strip between the trees at the side of the road, and I turned my body to lean on the steering wheel and looked into the future. All the other cars were slicked down, with every driver gazing like an eagle. The green Mercedes expanded. I only wanted Liska.

The road was pure and swift, and the rumbling of the wheels was a nagging chafe, spoiling my desire for sleep and urging me on, and I huddled down behind the wheel, determined that I would complete my mission, do what I could with the remainder of Liska's work and then plan the rest of my life from there.

56

■ Worn but not devoured, and longing for the sea, I arrived among the bungalows of Milltimber, having finished my third bottle of beer. Lanes angled between hedges and I tried to remember the way to Anna Lunken's house, not so easy since everything looked the same and the houses were hidden by trees. I slowed down, barely making any speed, careful not to disturb the insipid strain of suburban silence, the headlights shining on the hedges and gates that I passed. I had already made the plans for the rest of my life. A trip to the ferry, there to sail to Shetland and try once again where I had so badly failed before.

I parked the green Mercedes at the top of the road, next to the church and up against a hedge. In the heart of Anna Lunken's cul de sac, common age was visible. From the trees, pencils of moonlight shone on the driveways. I caught my breath and panted. To destroy any of Liska's paintings was an undertaking full of risk these days — but I'd worked myself into a fit and there was no going back.

> cf. Jules Pascin (1885-1930) American painter, draftsman and printmaker. Hanged himself in his Paris studio, upset by the reviews of his current show.

I glanced over the road and what did I see? A jeep on the gravel, and a row of perfect raised beds. This tidy Aberdeen suburb was relinquished to the most terrible silence where the houses looked out from behind the trees. I wondered what the residents might have done to deserve this locale, to be locked in those unbreathing, unsexual homes. The sign read Glengarse and I recognised the name as being the home of Anna Lunken. Gratefully I had arrived at the correct level of paradise. Anna Lunken's jeep was parked there, its pretty curves murdering the neighbour's hedge — but other than the cracks of light from behind the odd curtain, there was no sign of life, and I stopped to admire the house in its stultifyingly quaint setting.

Home, I thought, is the warm feeling of peace that comes from being right. Once I've destroyed Anna Lunken's Liska pictures then I'll be right and she'll be wrong again, I thought. The police will differ and her friends will differ — but I'll be out of her hair by then.

I walked into the shadow of Anna Lunken's back garden, and as I passed a waste pipe hissed with a flush of water from above. The wooden furniture in the back garden was so brand new, it still had the factory stickers across it. Liska had run across this garden once, with contracts under her arm.

I looked up to the top window where there was a closed curtain and I paused, stalled beside the house with a gloomy patience, as if there were a few more decisions to be made. I must have appeared crestfallen, staring at that back garden, remembering the way Liska had jumped the hedge and run down the steely bank of the lane, brimful of confidence in herself.

The back door was not locked and so I opened it and entered the kitchen, where I saw Anna Lunken's weirdo kettle. Everything was white and clean inside and I chose my weapon from the knife rack, a blade as sharp as ocean salt. A kitchen knife to cut still life, I thought — and it brought to mind all of the art that had been made and burned already — and a trumpet blew.

{YES!} Art is a waste of time. It is not good. The people who buy it are using it to decorate their walls. Art school may be satisfying but those kids could be making biscuits in there. The worst of it is that artists see themselves as doing something good! {YES!} The trumpet blew. {YES!} Liska had been right to deny the world her art — to keep it from the galleries and the following that danced around it. Mr Sharma and Paul Raytheon had been correct to follow Liska — to recognise what she was trying to do by holding the opinions that she did.

Because {YES!} that's what art does. It supersedes itself. And no generation knows precisely how to make art art, because art happens by itself. Art's generosity to the darkness of modern life is legendary. There is no reason for art to be overvalued and asked to wallow on our walls.

> cf. Mark Rothko : *Light Red Over Black* (1957) Oil on canvas. 'Millionaire friendly wall-paper.' (Simon Schama)

In Anna Lunken's living room art was represented fully. In the semi-circular canals of her wallet, there was always room for more art. What Anna Lunken owned was only good for destruction, and I recognised most of it. If it wasn't something I knew directly, I could certainly tell the style. Maybe you could call it the Originality School, in which everyone was original. When you're young you believe that a painting has to be good or bad — one or the other — but the truth is that art is an event — and as Liska knew, it didn't need to be good or bad for that.

Event. Yes. I raised the knife as I heard footsteps upstairs. The feet crossed the floor and I cut through the nearest painting — a crimson abstract of Liska's. The smell of the cut abstract reminded me of art shows — it reminded me of going to many different art shows and how I used to wonder at the inevitable pretence of using art as a way of making a living.

And what did I see at these shows?

Artists — either nervous or arrogant about how and why their work was bought and sold.

I cut through the picture properly, to make sure that there could be no hope for its reparation. I could make a career of this, I thought — or at least I could try. This kitchen knife was good and it sliced through Liska's picture so well that I didn't want to stop. The motion was gentle and bright, and I saw myself redeeming whole nations with my blade (I was clearly mad) — but Anna Lunken's knife was useful. The knife cut everything that it sliced. In the world of paper, stone, scissors, art was beaten by the knife, every time.

The last of Liska's painting lay on the floor in shreds and I felt better than ever. It was the one quality that art had always given me. Nothing could ever provide for that feeling — the externalising of your feelings into action — that's what gives artists such a base. It was blissful to simultaneously realise this and reclaim art from its kidnappers.

Once more the thump of footsteps, and I paused. Upstairs there was more art attached to the walls — Liska's work and that of others — nothing at all that couldn't be destroyed on the grounds of compassion alone.

I started up the stairs with the knife pointing forward and after several steps I heard voices. When I arrived on the top step I had a further choice of rooms. The door of one of the rooms, from where the voices came, was ajar enough to suggest something romantic from within — something friendly — people in bed.

Across the landing was more art and I waited, dimly aware of Liska. Liska was working her way out of a pool and along a branch of seaweed that grew up from a pipe. She whispered quiet commands and in the sight-hole in her skull was the glow of positive intention.

A laugh from along the corridor — Anna Lunken's laugh — and I pointed the knife towards the bedroom door. Liska trailed up the branches of weed. Her face softened, it was recognisable as her, but only by the hair. I walked to the end and stood beside the door.

These moments are great tests. If you put yourself in these situations often enough, you begin to realise that nothing can control the outcome. Instead of indecision you have the satisfaction of being able to act without fear.

Of course, to be in somebody's house and approaching their bedroom with a kitchen knife was further than most people get. If this level of madness has already kicked in then it's likely you're going to go all the way. Crime inspires this response. Car theft leads to entering houses and entering houses leads to damage of property. If things get in the way of damage of property, then people can be hurt.

The sounds of love came from within, but I wasn't quite ready for who or what. Even in Anna Lunken's bedroom there was a slight surprise in store.

It was young Alex Lash — he and Anna Lunken in the bed. That kid — he must have been 20 years old — and I walked in with my knife. They recognised me at once, and made no effort to move.

"Guy," said Anna Lunken and pulled the sheets towards her neck.

Lash couldn't hide his fear. He glanced towards the window and began gibbering, but I hissed for them both to shut up.

"I want that picture," I said, displacing my vexation to the very tip of Anna Lunken's kitchen knife.

"Liska's picture?" asked Anna Lunken, her knuckles gripping the covers.

Even in the direst circumstances humanity feigns a strange wriggling motion in its attempt to live another day — it's like a mental reflex. Anna Lunken must have known by this time that Liska's pictures were going to be destroyed but she still had it in her mind to stall the process. The difficulty was that there was a portrait of Liska right above Anna Lunken's bed — Liska's face, threatening to imprint itself further on me. Liska looked upon the lovers and then at myself and I couldn't think of any way of avoiding her dying once again.

"Liska's pictures," I said. "That's what I'm here for. Including that one."

Above Anna Lunken's bed, above Anna Lunken's head, the only

213

self-portrait Liska ever painted. Liska's eyes were iced, her lips were closed, her chin slightly raised as if in challenge.

The Lunken face didn't change — she'd known the first moment that she'd seen me what I wanted. The Lash kid was motionless but at any moment he might try the hero — and I waved my knife, determined to be frightening. I'd never wanted to see Anna Lunken again when Liska and I took the boat to Shetland, and I knew I was always going to be judged as being in the wrong for everything that had happened — but I had an aim — the eradication of my lover's work.

Lash was chancing glances around the room — for weapons I guessed. He looked at his shoes and wished that he was wearing them. He even looked at the bedside lamp that I may be decked with it. Anna Lunken tried that dreamy hypnotic stare that she used on works of art she wanted, trying to succour me with pity.

Seconds were all I had. Lash's shoulders emerged from the covers. He was delightfully all bones, and he said something, it sounded like a cat's meow. They both grabbed what they could and slid to the side, allowing me to step on to the mattress and gently put the knife into Liska's face. I let fall the reins and the canvas tore and for a moment I withdrew to see Liska's face one last time. Anna Lunken said nothing while I cut.

It was the very last part of Liska's life and I realised that I was about to shred it. There was a frame and a canvas there, but no art — that had gone forever. I had the knife and was ready to carry out Liska's final mischievous notion, by destroying a self-portrait that she'd done, that she never wished for anyone else see, far less buy or sell.

I pulled the picture away to allow myself a better grip — and I offer you now, those that remain neutral to this, the chance to look away.

We've seen a lot destroyed so far, and there is still some more to go. We've burned and slashed many a painting and killed a few ducks to boot. So much has been done now that if you like, you can be spared the final cut. It was a tough moment but maybe that's because finishing is the hardest thing. To get to the end of your work and proclaim it done — it really is a difficult thing to do.

Look away now!

57

☐ The next morning was wet and clear in Aberdeen. A pale multi-coloured dappling covered the granite. At the harbour-mouth one rudder slowed and the ferry keeled to face the north, and the feeling was magnificent, as if I were allowed to look at my hometown one last time, broadside.

I had slept the night in the car and it lay parked on Pocra Quay. I guess the car was the last thing I said goodbye to. Facing the turrets of the town and the plain rail of the horizon, just in that second, clarity popped up and the blessings of my sins filled me, as pungent as an armful of freshly cut grass.

No one's espousing the values of naivety — it's quite the opposite. The world I looked upon from the ferry was built by honest people, and who could deny them a right to the art on their walls? Not me, I thought, and that was why I had to go.

What were my sins?

Stealing Mr Sharma's Mercedes had been a sin. Never steal an art patron's Mercedes. Of the various paths taken by man, this is the one most likely to inspire damnation. Strike a bargain, come to a covenant, concede, accept and recognise your patron's general argument, but never steal his Mercedes. Such a theft will upset the already tangled process of natural evolution as the art patron will never be able to say anything nice about your work again. Your average art patron (higher ratio of body volume to body surface — body parts and head of a gorilla — genitals of a whale) cannot adapt to any other vehicle than a Mercedes, and will feel trapped and helpless in the lower organism of a public bus.

What other sins did I commit?

I forsook — nice Biblical word that — I forsook the comfort of a paid job to be an artist, abandoning human ritual for the excesses of drawing and painting. I attempted to atone for this by carrying out Liska's wishes, by staying around after she had died, to make sure her legacy was safely destroyed. Paid work is a thermal reservoir of comfort where the wretched relax while artists and writers do all the real work. In that reservoir of lunch, pension plans and free pens, I could not settle because — and I should be frank and plain — I could not take the boredom.

I stood on the deck of the Shetland ferry, amused that I had gone so far only to end up back there. I was glad I'd stayed around to see Liska's paintings demolished and I maintain that she would have enjoyed it. She would have been delighted that some of her work had been reclaimed from the art-liking crowd and pleased that they hadn't been allowed to go on the market.

Then, as ever, I wanted to be with Liska. From the front of the ferry I tried to work out where Liska had jumped, that one irrecoverable point that led to her new resting place, but the sea was eternal, a pale grey nothing. The air was marginally warmer than it had been the previous month, but its essential roughness was the same.

Inside the body of the boat, the bar was not the same. Around the walls of the bar and on the old banquettes, the islanders sat in a pucker of dark beards while their dogs worried like children beneath the chairs. Men and wives supported each other on the horizontal retail of the sea bar and the heavy musculature of Viking lorry-drivers blocked the fruit machines. Different bar staff, similar set up, so I began to drink and waited to see who would speak to me before I left for the bottom of the sea.

But nobody spoke to me — and so there was no redemption and no life-saving remedy. The barman wasn't even friendly and so the unmistakable signature of the rum began to depress me, and I knew less of my surroundings and more of my intentions.

There were no notes nor final words, no insistent urge to shirk or lounge. I saw Liska in the radiant calm of her new home as if she were standing on the edge of some peaceful and world-ending wave. Human voices spoke in the bar and others sang country songs on the speakers — country feelings, country people, and I had nothing more to say than —

Any more sins?

None at all, I answered.

I may leave through the waters drunkly, I thought, but I'll do so without sin.

In my pockets I had several scraps of painting ready for Liska as a present. The scraps I had taken had been of a flower and had been destroyed in Mr Sharma's studio. Like the many flowers Liska had painted, this had been a succulent, one that had lived underground. The tops of the flower's transparent leaves poked through the sand like pebbles, and light passed down their corpuscles and into the bulb. If you looked at that painting you could see that Liska had given the flower a facial expression and that a flower really has a face.

It was not a joke. Forget the modern menace and open the door to something that in rational terms is insecure and speculative. You would look at that painting and think to yourself: the flower is like I am. The roots reminded the viewer of a lung, or of the branches of a tree, the point being that these were dependable shapes, forms that protect everything. This ideal of equilibrium had existed in the studio, but the painting had been seen by several people and their eyes had broken it. I had destroyed the painting for this reason — but I'd kept several scraps for the sea — just in case Liska should wish a keepsake.

58

■ The warmth of the water took me by surprise. Whether it was the normal temperature for the sea at the close of winter or the chemical wake of the ferry, I wasn't sure, although I can safely say that it was warm. I was buoyant for a moment, and I placed my consciousness in the safekeeping of the fact that there was no way back and that I had begun to make my final journey.

Losing air to sorrow, I remembered a few books I'd wanted to write, thought of the parents one last time, wondered if Heery had found my computer and saved my work — and in the trance of my dying, my legs began to kick less ardently.

Once bled of air I dropped towards the trenches and sinks, the boundaries and transformed faults that have never been seen by man nor sub.

I left the North Sea downward, my final memory being a children's project we'd done at school, something on the fishing industry. I loved that school and I loved that project, and I had loved being a little boy. Nothing had been as good as being a little boy, I remembered, and that project had meant so much to me.

I sank through a scattering of fish, dropping until the particles of my eyes peeled away and I was gazing into the dead glacial flour of the deep. In my final memory, I saw myself seated at a small desk in a classroom with other boys and girls. Our feet were in new sandals and our pencils, rulers and sharpeners sat in formation across maps of the coast. There were pictures of various boats on the chalkboard and I held a booklet called <u>Fraserburgh Means Fish</u>.

"These are cod," said the teacher, "— and that is herring."

At one time that was the most important thing I had ever heard. When you are small, facts are vital, new and stirring, and details make life complete. On my desk I explored the coast which was drawn before me in the lead of my own pencil. The teacher spoke and the children paused in wonder.

"Trawler nets are so-called because they *trawl* the sea and catch the fish," she said.

Marine diatoms drifted from the deep and I weakly tried to recall the remaining part of the lesson. I was sure it would come to me.

The first ridge of mud was laden with strange spars of rotten wood which ran across the bed of the North Sea. There was nobody there but a bunch of squid, brushing up on their own fieldwork.

Below these guys, a bank of sediment formed a beach shaped by undersea waves and an orbital motion in the current produced a flow that set me towards a nest of fragments or flakes that filled my mouth. The canyon that opened before me was dammed by a bank of mud that I ran against and which pulled me to a halt. A current rippled and bubbles rose up from the mud, and when the current became strong enough to free me, I slid along the sea floor, coasting feet-first towards a trough which dipped further into the planet surface.

Some of the particles I passed had eyes. The ocean's gorge was wide and I saw heads down below, eyes with crosses through the centre of their lenses, and the bubbling swim bladder of something that had seen me and floated back into the dark — a free-floating bulb of a fish with a neuromast. I tried to follow the neuromast down the current by moving my arms or hands, but I hadn't the energy.

As I settled, tiny bone lipids ate into my waist. I recalled the night before, or seemed to have a dream in which I clutched my trousers in the two bony branches of my hands and said that I must replace them.

The neuromast fish was staring at me with its bulbous eyes, two dim sacs of light concentrated at the base of its dorsal fins.

I hung in the gel for an age. Light spoiled the shapes of the darkness and an enzyme layer formed in the mile of sea ahead of me. When I began to move again, many hours later, I saw a broad strip of bunkers filled with grey sands, and in slow stretches of my ligaments I began towards them, a solitary husk of limited mobility on a dark plain of misshapen mud. One of my legs had attracted a weird decapod crustacean which used a set of depressible teeth to hang inside the refuse of my knee.

Traps and trawl cod ends — scraps of Fraserburgh net and the death of fish boxes — the familiar green nozzle of what was once a bottle of Baal's Beer stuck in a tarp of sand — the pitching and rolling of water as it moved back and fore with the deepest of tides.

Ice fish perched on the sponge of the sand on elongated pelvic fins. As I slowed, many more beings appeared in tripods, breathing in the zooplankton. There was nobody there, but I kept going.

It was the benthic realm. Species here — myself included — lived in physical contact with the bottom of the sea. Many were not mobile, like the megafaunal browsers that eyed me with an impartial hunger. While I made my way forward, following the slow-moving gelatinous comb jellies, tubular mouths opened slowly in the mud.

Down there I reached Liska — when bloated and white — when headfirst and in the clearance of the darkness — I reached her. She looked like a tattered canvas herself, and she complimented me as I approached.

As for the rest, this prose has left the world you read it in and can no more make sense than the shreds we left on Anna Lunken's bedroom floor.

It's not that I wouldn't like to tell you what it was to be with Liska in our final and immortal high — because I would — it's only that down here, our language is understandably so removed, you'd have to join us to find out.

THE END